THE VIRGIN'S DANCE

AN OLDER MAN/YOUNGER WOMAN ROMANCE

MICHELLE LOVE

HOT AND STEAMY ROMANCE

CONTENTS

About the Author	vii
Sign Up to Receive Free Books	ix
Blurb	xi
1. Chapter One	1
2. Chapter Two	6
3. Chapter Three	13
4. Chapter Four	17
5. Chapter Five	25
6. Chapter Six	29
7. Chapter Seven	34
8. Chapter Eight	40
9. Chapter Nine	47
10. Chapter Ten	55
11. Chapter Eleven	73
12. Chapter Twelve	84
13. Chapter Thirteen	90
14. Chapter Fourteen	100
15. Chapter Fifteen	108
16. Chapter Sixteen	114
17. Chapter Seventeen	118
18. Chapter Eighteen	123
19. Chapter Nineteen	129
20. Chapter Twenty	130
21. Chapter Twenty-One	136
22. Chapter Twenty-Two	144
23. Chapter Twenty-Three	149
24. Chapter Twenty-Four	156
25. Chapter Twenty-Five	161
Sign Up to Receive Free Books	163
Preview of While You Were Gone	164
Chapter One	168
Chapter Two	175

Chapter Three	183
Chapter Four	191
Chapter Five	198
Other Books By This Author	207
About the Author	209
Copyright	211

Made in "The United States" by:

Michelle Love

© Copyright 2020 – Michelle Love

ISBN: 978-1-64808-123-1

ALL RIGHTS RESERVED. No part of this publication may be reproduced or transmitted in any form whatsoever, electronic, or mechanical, including photocopying, recording, or by any informational storage or retrieval system without express written, dated and signed permission from the author

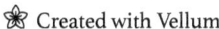 Created with Vellum

ABOUT THE AUTHOR

Mrs. Love writes about smart, sexy women and the hot alpha billionaires who love them. She has found her own happily ever after with her dream husband and adorable 6 and 2 year old kids.
Currently, Michelle is hard at work on the next book in the series, and trying to stay off the Internet.
"Thank you for supporting an indie author. Anything you can do, whether it be writing a review, or even simply telling a fellow reader that you enjoyed this. Thanks

facebook.com/HotAndSteamyRomance

instagram.com/michellesromance

SIGN UP TO RECEIVE FREE BOOKS

Sign Up to Receive Free E-Books and Audiobook Codes.

Would you like to read **The Unexpected Nanny, Dirty Little Virgin** and **other romance books** for **free**?

You can sign up to receive these free e-books and audiobooks by typing this link into your browser:

https://www.steamyromance.info/free-books-and-audiobooks-hot-and-steamy/

Or this one:

https://www.steamyromance.info/the-unexpected-nanny-free/

BLURB

It took me by surprise, but now I can't stop thinking about him.

Pilot Scamo. World-famous photographer. Billionaire. Drop-dead gorgeous man. Broken man. He's nearly twice my age but I've never felt this connection before ... I feel it everywhere, my heart, my head, my body. It's like electricity when he touches me, kisses me, When he makes passionate love to me. He's intoxicating and all I want now is to hold him, Protect him, love him. Will they let us be? We both have so much dark history, so many people against us. I'll fight for you, Pilot, even if it costs me everything ... I'll fight for you...
This book is a full-length standalone novel with a guaranteed HEA, no cliffhanger and plenty of steam. Exclusive bonus content included.

In the cutthroat world of contemporary ballet, young principal dancer Boheme Dali is already a trailblazer. The first Indian American woman to become principal at a major New York ballet company, Boh hides the tragedy of her past as she works tirelessly to become prima ballerina and make her mark on the world.

What she doesn't expect is to fall in love. But when world-renowned photographer Pilot Scamo, heir to a vast fortune, comes into her life, she discovers a soulmate and a creative partner like no other.

A passionate, sensual affair begins as Boh and Pilot begin to work on a project which will bring them both plaudits and fame, but at the center of it all are two people, both traumatized and damaged, who discover something beautiful.

Soon enough though, dark forces swirl around the happy couple, and a serious of tragic and horrifying events threaten to destroy their happiness. Can Boh and Pilot's love survive everything working against them and can they find their happy ever after?

∼

New York City

September

She stood on the roof, looking down at the stream of diamonds and pearls, the headlights and taillights of the cars flowing through Manhattan's streets. She liked the way it moved like a flood of sparkles beneath her, like the theater lights flickered when she was dancing.

Her feet scuffed along the concrete wall that surrounded the roof. It had been so easy to get up here. She smiled. Normally heights would make her stomach knot up and her legs shake, but not tonight. No, tonight was a command performance, and she was ready. She stood en pointe, ready to begin as the music in her head began to play.

Glissade, jeté, pas de bourrée, brisé. Along the wall to the far corner of the building. She had chosen this particular building because of its significance to her. To him. She could have gone to the ballet company's own building in Tribeca, but no, this building was her choice for her final performance.

In this building, three floors below her, he was fucking his latest whore. She counted—this was his sixth since the divorce, since he'd left her with nothing. Fuck you, Kristof, just fuck you. She'd enjoyed posting the letter to the New York Times, detailing Kristof's ill-treatment of her, the drug-taking, the philandering. Fuck him and fuck that ballet company. She was the prima, she would always be the prima ...

She stood, en pointe, at the corner of the wall, and spread out her arms gracefully, her fingers perfectly placed, preparing for her *grand jeté*.

The big leap.

She smiled, bent her knees, and took off.

CHAPTER ONE

New York City

One year later

Pilot Scamo closed his eyes and counted to ten, willing his phone to stop buzzing. Don't give in to her, don't answer the phone. To his relief, the phone fell silent, and he breathed out a sigh.

Looking up, he saw a table of young women staring at him and giggling. He smiled at them, and sure enough, a moment later, one of them dared to come over.

"Mr. Scamo?"

He stood and shook the young woman's hand. "Hey there." She flushed red with pleasure. He posed for a selfie with her and signed her notepad. She thanked him and went back to her table.

He was used to the attention. His name was well-known in celebrity circles now, thanks to his skill behind the camera.

Pilot Scamo, the son of a billionaire Italian city banker and an American feminist, was nearly forty now, but age had not withered his incredible looks. Intense green eyes, dark olive skin, and an unruly mop of wild dark curls meant he was catnip to women—and men—and people assumed he would be someone who slept around.

His ex-wife always assumed he was fucking the models and celebrities he shot for Vogue and Cosmo and so she had taken a myriad of lovers in their fifteen-year marriage. Pilot? Not once. He had been steadfastly faithful to Eugenie, even as she screwed her way through her Upper East Side friends' husbands, then his friends, his colleagues … even his ex-best friend Wallis. Wally had been drunk, and devastated afterward, but Genie had crowed in Pilot's face.

Her cruelty had been her own way of loving him.

But, even now, three years after he'd finally had enough and divorced Genie, she still kept him on a string, using his kind nature against him, always playing the victim, the narcissist in her unleashed. She had been desperate to cling to him, proud to be on the arm of such a beautiful man, the envy of every woman.

Her cocaine habit had grown out of control, and now the rail-thin blonde was heading for some sort of crisis. But God help me, I can't be part of it, Pilot thought now. He rubbed his eyes and checked his watch. Nelly was late, of course. His old college buddy, now the publicist for one of America's most prestigious ballet companies, was irreverent, gossipy, and the complete opposite of Genie—the two women loathed each other and made no secret of it, and so he hadn't seen Nelly for nearly seven years. When she'd called him out of the blue and arranged a lunch at Gotan on Franklin Street, Pilot had been delighted.

He saw her now, barreling through the door, her messenger bag knocking a glass off a table, her musical laugh as she apologized to the server who came to help. Pilot grinned as he watched Nelly charm the young man, then she was hugging Pilot. "Gorgeous boy, how are you?"

Pilot kissed her cheek. "I'm good, thank you, Nel. Glad to see you again."

They sat down and Nelly unwound her scarf from her neck, studying him. "You look stressed. Maleficent still bugging you day and night?"

Pilot had to laugh. Nelly's disdain for Eugenie was biting and hilarious—or would be if it wasn't so on the money. "You know Genie."

"Unfortunately." Nelly grimaced. "She showed up to one of the company's benefits the other day with a dude who could have been your mini-me."

A curl of unease crept through Pilot's body. Jesus, really, Genie? She was determined to humiliate him at every turn. Nelly noticed his expression and her own softened. "Hey, for what it's worth, she was a laughing stock."

"That doesn't help." Pilot blew out his cheeks and fixed a smile on his face. "But let's get back to you. It's so good to see you, Nel."

She reached over and squeezed his hand. "You too, Pil. God, you get better looking every year—if only I was born liking dudes, I'd do you sideways."

Pilot snorted with laughter. "Sideways? How exactly would that work?"

"You dare to question me?" Nelly grinned. "How's work?"

Pilot's smile faded. "Slow. I have an exhibit coming up at MOMA, to benefit the Quilla Chen Foundation ... Grady Mallory offered it to me, but I haven't got anything. Not anything." He tapped his head. "Nothing is going on up here; the juice isn't flowing. I spend my days just wandering around the city, hoping something will trigger an idea."

"Hobo."

Pilot smiled. "Brainless hobo, at the moment."

"Well, I may be able to help."

They were interrupted then by the waiter who took their order, grilled cheese for Pilot, a cauliflower and tahini sandwich for Nelly, a lifelong vegetarian. As Pilot sipped his coffee, he raised his eyebrows at Nelly. "So?"

"The Company is struggling," she said matter-of-factly. "Since Oona's suicide, and the crap in the paper about Kristof, our funding has dropped significantly."

"I read about that ... so that stuff about Kristof isn't true?"

"Oh, no," Nelly shook her head, "it's all true. He is a junkie and a cheating asshole, but he's also a genius artistic director. Really, he couldn't be more clichéd if he tried, but Oliver Fortuna is determined to keep hold of him."

"Who is Fortuna?"

Nelly smiled. "Our founder. God bless him, he's wonderful, and he's intensely loyal." She sighed. "Too loyal, sometimes. Anyway, I digress. We were talking about ways to up our profile without referencing Kristof's past, and a photographic exhibit of our dancers, shot by one of the best photographers in the work—you—would be a great start. Then, we're working towards a major performance of work, called La Petite Morte. Kristof is putting it together—it's an excerpt from erotic ballets with a dark twist."

Pilot was nodding, but he wasn't enthused. "I'm happy to help but it's been done, recently too."

"Wait until you see our dancers—there are one or two of them who transcend ballet. That's all I'll say now because I want you to find your muse in our company. Pilot, you were the first person I thought of for this—I've seen you get that glint in your eye when something or someone inspires you." She squeezed his cheek, grinning. "Trust me on this—you will find it at NYSMBC."

. . .

LATER, as he walked home to his penthouse flat, he wondered about the job. The New York State and Metropolitan Ballet Company. He knew very little about dance, but Nelly had been their chief of publicity for many years, and he'd occasionally photographed their shows for them.

Kristof Mendelev was another matter. Pilot's dealings with the man had only ever been negative—Mendelev had been one of Eugenie's myriad lovers and had boasted about it whenever Pilot had been to one of their functions. He knew the ex-ballet dancer was loathed by his colleagues, but like Nelly had told him, Kristof was a genius on the ballet stage. Feted by every major ballet company around the world, Kristof knew his worth.

"He's the reason we're struggling cash-wise," Nelly had told Pilot. "His salary is six figures, but he has to submit to weekly drug-testing. That's the one unbreakable condition of his employment. So far—he's clean."

Pilot had told Nelly he would happily photograph the dancers for the company but he didn't hold faith that it would be the key to unlocking his inspiration. When he got home, he checked his voicemails. Grady Mallory, just checking in. Pilot deleted that message guiltily. One message from his mom, Blair, asking him to call her. Three from his younger half-sister Romana, herself an up-and-coming photographer, and finally, seven messages from Eugenie, each more hysterical than the last.

Don't give in to her. Don't call her back.

Pilot sighed and flicked through his contacts, pressing the dial button. After a second, he heard her voice—and smiled. "Hey, little sis," he said, his tone warm and loving, "what gives?"

CHAPTER TWO

Boheme Dali battered her shoes against the stone wall, trying to break them in. She thought she had done so last night, hours of bending and stretching the shoes, but, as always with new shoes, they'd wrecked her feet after only one ballet class.

She looked up as a female voice called her name, and smiled. Grace Hardacre, one of the guest performers this year, came to sit down by her in the corridor outside the studio. "Hey, Boh."

"Hey yourself. How's mentoring going?" Grace was mentoring an apprentice of the ballet company's in addition to performing with them.

Grace smiled. "Lexie is incredible," she said warmly, "and such a sponge. I tell her one thing and she gets it."

Boheme smiled. She remembered what it had been like to be an apprentice, even one with her talent; she was still put through the ringer by her tutor, former prima ballerina, Celine Peletier, who was now her champion and a formidable teacher at the company. It had made her the dancer she was today.

Grace nodded at her shoes. "The one constant in ballet—painful shoes. New?"

"Yup." Boheme grimaced as she saw blood in the toe of them. "God, Liquid Skin, here I come." She dragged the tube of liquid bandage from her bag.

Grace looked sympathetic. "Ouch."

Boheme shrugged. "But necessary. Anyway, what brings you over here?" She sucked in a breath as she applied the liquid to her toes.

"The douche wishes to see me about the workshop. I think he wants me on his side about what ballets he wants to do."

"Ah. They're still fighting over The Lesson?"

"Yup. Liz thinks it's misogynist and too violent, whereas Kristof says that's the point of the whole sex and death thing he's got going on."

Boheme rolled her eyes. "I hate to say this, but I kind of get where he's coming from." She bent over as far as she could and blew on her toes.

"Me too, but Liz argues Mayerling or La Sylphide cover the same ground."

"Well, she's right, but isn't that point of this workshop? We're doing three excerpts from three different stories." Boh sighed. "Well, whatever. It's not like we haven't plenty of tragic ballets to choose from. Although I have to admit, I'm relieved not to have to do Romeo and Juliet again."

Grace chuckled. "You've always hated that one. People love it."

"It's not a love story," Boh said, "it's a stupid teen angst story."

"Philistine."

"Boring."

They both laughed and Grace help Boh get to her feet. "Come on, let's grab something to eat before we go home."

Boh and Grace shared a walk-up apartment in Brooklyn and

had done so since they were both in the corps de ballet. Now that they were both senior dancers, they could have afforded their own places, but they enjoyed living with each other and saw no reason to change.

They ate at a small diner on the way to the subway, then huddled down together as the train took them home. September and the heat of the New York summer had quickly faded and as fall began, the leaves were falling and a cold wind from the north was swirling around the city.

AT HOME, their cat, Beelzebub, a darkly malevolent tabby, was waiting for them to feed him, wandering between their legs, yelling until Boh dumped a bowl of kibble on the kitchen floor for him. "Fiend," she said fondly, scratching his ears as he ate his food.

Grace had a date, and so, after commandeering the bathroom for an hour, she called goodbye to Boh, who was reading in her room. The apartment was silent after Grace left, and Boh reveled in the peace of it. She loved being alone, away from other people, the long hours of exercise and practice a strain on her introverted side

She loved ballet, every part of it except the public side. Boh had been raised to be quiet, the silent child at the dinner table, the only-speak-when-spoken-to daughter. The youngest of five, Boh had often been forgotten by her wayward parents, who only had children because it was expected of them in their Indian American family. The moment she was sixteen, Boh had taken the money she had saved from her part-time job at the local Dairy Queen and caught a bus to New York City. She had lived on fellow dancers' couches until she was accepted into her ballet school, then stayed in the dorm rooms, where she had met Grace.

Now in her own place, her family a distant memory, Boh was as content as she had ever been—apart from one glaring thing. Lately, she had experienced fatigue for many days in a row. Days turned into weeks, and finally, last week she had been to see her doctor. She had anemia, probably, her doctor told her, hereditary. "A mild version, thank goodness, and we can treat you." The doctor smiled kindly at her as she read through her notes. "I already know the answer to this, Boh, but could you see yourself taking some time off?"

They had both laughed, but they both knew there was zero chance of that. "I'll take any pills, eat anything you say I should, but that's the one thing I can't do. I will get as much rest as I can, I promise." Boh told her, and the doctor had to be satisfied with that.

Boh got up now and went to run a bath. She thought herself lucky that her naturally introverted nature meant she rarely went out at night, preferring to stay home and read or watch movies. She and Grace would sometimes cook for each other, healthy, made-from-scratch meals from recipes they found on the Internet, otherwise a usual diet of salmon or chicken with steamed vegetables was their mainstay.

Despite the rumors of eating disorders plaguing the ballet world, it was less prevalent than expected and the NYSMBC had strict policies on nutrition. "Fit, healthy bodies of appropriate weight for age and height" was the mantra. When a dancer was suspected of developing a disorder, they were given three strikes to help combat it, and support to beat it. If the dancer didn't do their part, after three sessions with the company counselor, they were dismissed from the company and sent to a treatment center. The company's chief executive, Liz Secretariat, an exprima, enforced that rule fiercely, and chastised any teacher who made the dancers question their body shape.

Of course, it didn't mean the dancers could gorge themselves, but now, when Boh broke off a large piece of dark chocolate and put it on a plate to enjoy as she soaked in the bath, she didn't feel guilty about it. She downed two of her prescribed iron tablets with some orange juice and grabbed her old half-buried-beneath-paperbacks copy of her company guidelines. She still didn't know whether she was required to report her illness if it wasn't serious. She would rather not. It would just mean the company watching her closely and she could do without that right now.

She wished Kristof, the company's art director, would make up his mind about which ballets to perform. It made rehearsals stressful when they were running through six or seven different combinations to vastly different music. All of the dancers' feet were wrecked, but Kristof seemed to work Boh harder than the rest. While they caught their breath, he would tell Boh to run through a set of leaps and jumps, basic steps that even the apprentices knew.

After the sessions, he would keep her longer to tell her about every single step she had performed, what was wrong with it, what was wrong with her. Boh had a thick skin and she would automatically filter out the nonsense and concentrate on the stuff that she could learn from.

Of course, when Kristof was in an extra-spiteful mood, even her thick skin couldn't escape his barbs. That, she knew, stemmed from her refusal to sleep with him. More than once he had come onto her, and every time she said no. It wasn't just that she had no interest in him sexually, but the thought of his hands on her body made her feel sick.

She knew some of her fellow dancers found him attractive, and looking at the man with an unbiased eye, she knew he was a handsome man. Dark hair, dark brown eyes, a square, strong jaw … yes, Kristof Mendelev was a catch.

But she loathed his personality, his arrogance, even though

his high opinion of his own talent was justified. Boh was so aware of the important of confidence tempered with humility that she couldn't abide conceit.

Serena, her fellow dancer and nemesis, would scoff at her. "You're too soft, Dali. This is ballet—it doesn't get more cutthroat than this."

"And yet, still, I made principal without having to resort to being a bitch, Serena," she would shoot back to the amusement of the other dancers.

Her hated of Serena went deeper than being rivals for the leading roles. Boh knew she had the edge—but so did Serena, and that made the other woman antagonistic. Not only that, but Boh suspected Serena of being racist. Boh was the first Indian American to become principal in their ballet company, and the company had made much in the media of her ascendance. Serena, an Upper East Side princess, had mocked the interviews and photo shoots, but Boh knew it was only out of jealousy.

Serena was a thorn in her side but not a big one. As Boh soaked in the tub, she tried to concentrate on her book—the new Paul Auster—but found her mind wandering. Today she had received a letter from her oldest sister, Maya, telling her that their father was seriously ill and not likely to live another six months.

Boh tested her heart and felt nothing. Nothing for the man who'd ignored her for the first seven years of her life, and then, on her eighth birthday, the day they had moved into a new apartment and she had her own room for once, the day he had crept into her room for what he would call their "Special Secret Time."

No, she felt nothing for the man who had abused her. She had told only one person—Maya—who had slapped her face and told her never to tell. Boheme knew, at that moment, that her father had done the same thing to her sister.

Bastard.

She had written back to Maya.

I'm sorry for the pain it causes the rest of you, but really, he gets what he deserves. You know why.

Boh.

There had been no reply and now Boh pushed the memories of her father away. You, she thought, you are the reason I have no heart, no passion for a man. You.

She hauled herself out of the cool water and studied her naked body in front of the mirror. Tall, lean, with skin the color of milky coffee, she nevertheless had full breasts, something Serena mocked her for too, but she never worried that she didn't fit the preferred dancer body type. It wasn't such a big deal, nowadays.

She dried herself off and changed into her worn but comfortable pajamas, slipping into bed and switching off the lamp. It was only 10 p.m. but she didn't care. Sleep was ambrosia to her, especially now. God, I am middle-aged at twenty-two, she thought to herself, but soon her eyes closed and she fell into a peaceful sleep, woken only by Beelzebub padding his paws onto her back in the early hours.

"You little asshole," she said, then smiled as he curled up on the pillow next to her and immediately stretched his leg over her face. She removed it gently and kissed his tiny paw. "You're the only man for me, Beez," she whispered, then closed her eyes and slept until her alarm sounded at seven a.m. the next morning.

CHAPTER THREE

"I can't remember—have you been inside this building before?" Nelly asked Pilot as he arrived with his Polaroid camera—he was old school when it came to initial scouting—two weeks after their lunch in the city. He'd moved things around, avoiding calls from Grady Mallory until he could no longer put it off. He'd had to make something up on the fly to tell Grady. "It's a study of the human body in movement," he said. "I'm visiting with the New York State and Metro Ballet to see their ballerinas at work.

He didn't blame Grady for sounding less than enthusiastic. Ballet dancers in movement had been done before, many, many times, but Grady, being the nice guy that he was, nevertheless thanked Pilot for his ideas.

Pilot felt bad about his lack of direction. "Look, Gray, I promise I'll come up with something spectacular."

"I have faith," Grady had told him. Pilot hoped he could repay that faith.

Following Nelly into the ballet company's building, he shook his head. "No, not this one, but the old one down on Bleecker."

"Ha, yeah, that's a story. That building was just condemned

... asbestos. We dodged a bullet there, selling it before it was discovered. Anyway, where do you want to start? Do you want to meet the dancers or just look in on a class?"

"Just look in, if that's all right. I just need to see who I'm going to be shooting."

"In that case," Nelly directed him into the elevator, "there's a mixed class you should see. Principals down to apprentices. Celine likes to hold a two-hour long class on Monday mornings which is more about fine-tuning than it is rehearsing for anything specific. Very good for building comradery in the company. Everyone loves it, as you can imagine, although they're all terrified of Celine."

Pilot grinned. His own mother was a strident, effusive, strong woman, and he'd inherited a love of powerful women—powerful, not manipulative. "How is the comradery?"

Nelly laughed. "What you would expect. For the most part, they're a friendly bunch, but there's always one or two assholes."

"Who should I look out for?"

Nelly chuckled. "I shouldn't say."

"Go on, gossip a little."

She sighed. "Serena. A Grade 1 uber-bitch. Fantastic dancer, of course, but a harridan. Jeremy can be a diva."

"You play favorites?"

"I don't teach them so I can." She gave him a mischievous look. "Boh. You'll love Boh. Lexie, Grace, Vlad, Elliott, Fernanda ... look, most of them. Just look out for Serena, Jeremy, and maybe even Alex."

"Good info, thanks."

They stepped out of the elevator and Nelly pointed him towards the studio. "I told Celine to expect you."

Pilot chuckled. "You know me so well."

He opened the door to the studio a crack and caught the eyes of the fierce-looking woman inside. She nodded, unsmiling, and nodded her head to the front of the class.

Pilot slipped inside, his eyes sweeping over the dancers inside. A couple looked at him curiously, but most were focused on their practice. A young man, around Pilot's age, was playing the piano. He looked up and smiled at Pilot.

"And up, good. Arms lifted ... Lexie, extend, please ... beautiful. Alex, turn out ... good. Lovely stretch, Boh, well done. Double pirouette, no, Elliot, double. Thank you."

Pilot listened to her guiding her pupils through the class. He had to admit, the way they used their bodies to form shapes was beautiful and impressive. He squatted at the front and took some shots. A dancer with pale, red-gold hair in a tight bun on the top of her head caught his eye and smiled seductively, posing for him.

"Serena, pay attention to me and not Mr. Scamo, please, no matter how pretty he is."

Pilot gave a snort of laughter and Celine glared at him, winking to show she was kidding. He liked her immediately.

"Okay, and rest. Thank you. Well, as Serena has noticed, we have a visitor. For those of you who live under a rock, this is Pilot Scamo, photographer extraordinaire." Celine came over to shake Pilot's hand as the assembled group gave him a small round of applause. He felt his face flame—he never got used to being the center of attention.

"Hey everyone, listen, I'm just here to capture the action, so please, don't let me interrupt ..." Pilot's voice faltered as he saw her. The tall, athletic woman standing a little way behind a male dancer. She was looking at him shyly, her dark brown eyes large, her body all curves and yet athletic and toned. She was luminous. Pilot realized he was staring and quickly looked away. "Sorry, um, don't let me interrupt you."

Celine hid a smile. "You heard the man. Right, next combination. In fourth, then plié, relevé, plié …"

Pilot continued his shooting while the dancers practiced. After working at the barre, Celine had them showcase their leaps and jumps for him. "And, Boh, if you could finish for us with your triple pirouette and into arabesque."

At the end of the jetés, his girl stepped forward, all grace, and executed a flawless pirouette and finished in the classic pose of arabesque. Every line of her body was exquisite, down to the placement of her fingers. Pilot sucked in a deep breath.

He had found his muse.

4
CHAPTER FOUR

As Boh left the studio, she couldn't help glancing back at the man talking to Celine. The way he had looked at her ... if any other man had looked at her like that, she would have frozen, gotten distressed, and panicked. But this man ...

It was his eyes. Bright green, and large, his thick dark brows making them intense, dangerous, sensual. A line between his brows made it look as if he was frowning or troubled until he smiled. Then his entire face lit up, became boyish, almost beautiful. He was the sexiest man she had ever seen, and she felt it everywhere.

Lexie nudged her. "Somebody made an impression."

Boh grinned at her and lowered her voice. "So you noticed too?"

"Everyone noticed, Boh. It was almost a cartoon double-take he did. And he's gorgeous too."

"Old enough to be your father," Serena butted in, obviously listening to them as they made their way to the changing rooms. "And you, Dali, don't go thinking you're something special just because a man gave you the eye. He's a superstar—he's probably had more supermodels in the last week than you've had successful triple pirouettes."

"Serena, your bitch is showing." Fernanda, the mild-mannered guest dancer from Ecuador spoke then, and Serena flushed with anger, muttering something under her breath. Fernanda stopped and gripped Serena's shoulder. "What did you say?"

Serena smiled nastily. "You heard." She wrenched her shoulder from Fernanda's grip and stalked off. Boh sighed. Serena's attitude had gotten even worse lately, and she wondered why Fernanda had got involved. It wasn't like her. She looked questioningly at her friend now and Fernanda shrugged.

"Sometimes she just needs to hear shut the fuck up from someone new, you know."

Boh and Lexie laughed and Fernanda grinned. "Come on. We'll be late for Kristof."

AFTER THE NOISE of the class, the studio rang with silence as Pilot laid out his Polaroids on top of the piano and studied them. He noted down several of the dancers he'd like to photograph, choosing them for the clean lines of their bodies, but really, he was trying not to concentrate on the last three pictures.

Boheme. Boh. The way her body moved through the air, her curves made as gracefully as the pin-thin dancers. Strong, athletic, and almost otherworldly. He knew enough about ballet to know her body type wasn't the preferred willowy waif. Her body was all woman, the result of a finely tuned workout program, he guessed, along with a healthy appetite. He found her thrilling. Her poise and grace were reflected in the natural beauty of her face, devoid of make-up and with a fine, dewy sheen of sweat making the light sparkle from her ...

Calm down, man. Pilot sucked in a deep breath but his

stomach was in knots. The old feeling. When he knew he'd found someone who could radiate sensuality, strength, and above all artistry through his lens. He would gladly photograph the rest of the dancers for the company, to help with their publicity, but he would ask Boh to work with him for his exhibition.

He went to find Nelly, who was delighted he had enjoyed the class. "The dancers are astonishing," he said honestly, sitting down on her desk. "There were a few who really stood out ... here." He handed her a set of six Polaroids and she sorted through them, nodding.

"Grace, Lexie, Jeremy, Vlad, Fernanda, and Elliott. Oh." She looked up at him curiously and he knew what she was thinking. He grinned and handed her the last three Polaroids.

"I said they stood out. But there was one who blew the rest out of the water."

He saw Nelly's shoulders relax as she looked at the pictures of Boh. She nodded and smiled. "I knew it. I knew you would like her. She's something else."

"That she is," he said and Nelly chuckled.

"Crushing?"

Pilot pretended to look affronted. "Please, I'm a professional. I'm also a man, and who could blame me? But seriously ... I have a proposition."

Nelly gave him a mischievous grin. "God, we're not talking Pygmalion, are we? I already have Machiavelli on staff."

"Ha, no, not quite. Listen, I told you about the Chen Foundation exhibit?"

"You did ... ah, I see. You want Boh to be your muse?"

Pilot nodded. "If she'll agree. It would mean working around her ballet schedule, of course, and she may not want to put in the extra hours. I'll pay her, of course ... and on top of that, I'll do your publicity shots free of charge."

Nelly's eyes bugged. "No, Pilot, I couldn't ..."

"Look at my eyes," he said, with a grin, "If you can tell me you've seen me more excited about a project than this, I take it all back."

A slow smile spread across Nelly's face. "Okay, you're on ... if Boh agrees."

"Of course, absolutely. But I'll do your stuff for free anyway." It wasn't as if he needed the money and as far as Pilot was concerned, Nelly had given him his mojo back and there was no price on that.

Nelly looked at the clock. "Well, Boh's in with Kristof at the moment. I could pull her."

"No, don't interrupt her class."

Nelly snorted. "It would piss Kristof off though, and everyone would enjoy that. Come on, let's go see if we can steal her away."

Kristof Mendelev stared at Boh as she moved through the mime section of La Sylphide and then stopped her. "Boh, this isn't a sarcastic rendition, nor is it a cartoon. Subtly is key in this part of the dance. If you break out and make the audience laugh then you're doing a disservice to the sensuality of the moment."

Boh stood silently as he critiqued her then asked coolly, "Shall I try it again?"

"What else are we here for? Of course, try again."

She moved across the floor, her port de bras moving in graceful arcs, her feet moving swiftly across the floor, fast and staccato in the style made famous by the ballet's choreographer August Bournonville. Boh knew this ballet better than most of the others, having loved it since she was a child. She loved being the fairy, the sylph, and so her body bent and curved to every note of the music. This time she played the mime earnestly, reaching out with her love across the forest where the fairies dwelled, proclaiming her love for James, the hapless hero of the ballet. Vladimir, Boh's fellow principal, played James, moving with her, and Boh lost herself in the movements.

As she played out La Sylphide's dying moments, her focus shifted back into the room and she saw Pilot Scamo watching her.

"Okay, stop." Kristof was rubbing his head and glaring at Nelly. "Is there some reason for this intrusion? How is she—" he gestured rudely towards Boh, "—going to get any better if we keep being interrupted?"

Nelly didn't rise to the bait. "I told you about this earlier, Kris. Were you listening?"

But he wasn't listening now; he was staring at Pilot, who gazed back coolly. "Well, if it isn't Scamo." He said his name with accompanying jazz hands, mocking Pilot. Pilot's eyes looked dangerous and Boh shivered, but he didn't take the bait. Pilot's eyes met hers and softened and his mouth hitched up on one side.

"Miss Dali," he said, his tone respectful and admiring, "looked exquisite to me."

Boh flushed with pleasure and then a snigger went through the class until Kristof glared at them.

Kristof rolled his eyes. "What do you want?"

"We'd like to talk to Boh, please. In private."

"And it couldn't wait until after my class?"

"Obviously not." Nelly's voice took on a dangerous note and Kristof stared her down for a moment, obviously deciding whether to argue his case. Eventually he gave a sharp nod of the head to Boh, who stepped out gracefully of the troupe and came towards them, gathering her bag and towel, shooting an apologetic look at the rest of her class.

· · ·

Outside, Nelly introduced them. "Boheme Dali, meet Pilot Scamo. Not that he needs introducing."

"And after what I saw this morning, neither do you, Miss Dali." He shook her hand and smiled at her.

"It's Boh, please." Her voice was quiet and soft, musical. Nelly grinned at them both, obviously noticing the forming connection between them.

"Pilot," he said and Nelly patted his back.

"I'll leave you two alone to talk. Pilot has a very interesting proposition for you, Boh."

She disappeared and Pilot smiled at Boh. "Shall we take a walk? I don't much feel like having an audience." He nodded inside the dance studio where Kristof was watching them and Boh nodded, rolling her eyes.

"Good idea. I know somewhere we can go for some privacy."

She took him down to the bottom of the building and out of the kitchen area to a small courtyard. "No one comes down here much unless it's to smoke, but class is in session so we should have some privacy." She shivered a little at the cold breeze.

"Here." Pilot shrugged out of his jacket and put it around her shoulders. She smiled at him gratefully.

"Thank you." They sat down at one of the picnic benches. "It really is an honor to meet you, sir."

Pilot grinned. "My dad was 'sir,' Boh, I'm just Pilot. And likewise. Nelly told me you were special and I believe she underplayed that statement. You move like—" he cast around for the word, "—like water, like air ... Boh, Nell mentioned a proposition and here it is. I'm scheduled to work with the Quilla Chen Foundation for an exhibit at MOMA in six weeks. Before this morning, I had nothing. No juices were getting to my brain, no inspiration, no nothing. Then I saw you dance."

The Virgin's Dance 23

Boh's face was flaming red. Pilot Scamo was inspired ... by her? No way. No freakin' way. Pilot's name was known all over the world and he'd photographed some of the world's most beautiful women—Serena's jibe about him sleeping with supermodels came back to her.

"Mr. Scamo—"

"Pilot."

"Pilot—what exactly is it that you're asking me to do?" If this was a line to get her into bed—God help her but this gorgeous man wouldn't need a line—she would have to revise her good opinion of him.

"Work with me on this project. Obviously, we'll need a theme, and my ideas are at the very early stages. I'm sure you've seen the many, many ballet portraits that have been done already; photographers like Karolina Kuras or Alexander Yakovlev have produced some stunning work. So we need an original angle. I'd like to work with you and figure something out."

"In six weeks?"

Pilot nodded. "In six weeks we'd have to come up with a theme, get the costumes, find the settings." He smiled suddenly, a wide, boyish smile, and Boh felt her belly quiver with desire. Working closely together with this man for six weeks? Yes, please ...

"I'm in." She found herself saying and was reward by an even bigger, even sexier smile.

"Fantastic."

They swapped contact details and Boh smiled shyly at him. "I guess we're going to have to start right away."

"I guess so." His eyes dropped to her mouth for a split second and then he looked away, a faint spot of pink appearing on each of his cheeks. Boh realized he didn't want to look like a creep, but there was no denying the attraction between them. Still, this man was a professional and so was she.

But, at least, she thought later, after she'd said goodbye, I have a new friend. Ha, her body said to her, when was the last time you got wet over a friend?

Shut up. But she grinned to herself as she made her way back up to Kristof's class, feeling lighter than air at the thought of spending the next six weeks with Pilot Scamo.

CHAPTER FIVE

Pilot's good mood lasted until he got back to his apartment and saw his doorman shifting uncomfortably from foot to foot. "Mister Scamo," he said, "I'm sorry. She wouldn't take no for an answer. She's waiting upstairs."

Pilot sighed. "It's not your fault, Ben. It's okay."

Eugenie was sitting outside his apartment door and Pilot was grateful that he had never given in to her request for a key. "Why?" he had asked when Eugenie suggested it, "We're divorced, Genie."

She saw him now and held her hands out to him so he helped her up. She didn't let go of his hands, instead pressing them around her waist. "Darling."

Pilot gently extracted himself. "Genie, what are you doing here?"

Eugenie huffed. "Well, if you don't want to see me."

God, it was going to be one of those days. She really was the queen of passive-aggressiveness. "I'm working, Genie. As I said, what is it that you want?"

"To see you, obviously." She stroked a hand down his face

and it was all Pilot could do not to jerk his head away. He'd been there before and knew what the consequences of that would be. The half-moon scar next to right eye was evidence of Genie's rage when she was slighted. "I miss you, Pilot. More than you know."

Ah, Genie Ploy number three, he thought. The regretful ex. "Genie, you've been calling me nonstop and as I said, I'm working. You know what it's like when I have a project on."

He was hoping to keep the argument out in the hallway, but as one of his neighbors edged along the corridor, curious, and not being shy about it, Pilot opened his door and stepped back to allow Eugenie to enter. Damn it. He had been successfully keeping her away from his new life until now.

Genie walked into his apartment and smiled. "Ah, typical Pilot. Unorganized mess."

He shrugged. Eugenie liked everything in its place all the time; Pilot wanted his home to look lived in by a human, not an automaton. His walls were lined with bookshelves stuffed to the gills, his couch was old and battered and incredibly comfortable, his record player was on the floor with a stack of vinyl next to it. On the coffee table, a collection of mugs had varying degrees of old coffee or tea; a half-empty bottle of scotch, a notebook with ideas.

But Genie was wrong—Pilot knew where every single piece of his life fit in this place—it was his haven and he hated that she was in it, judging it, sneering at it.

"Like I said, many times now, I'm working, so—" He made a motion for her to say what she had to say. Genie half-smiled. She was looking even thinner these days. Always slim, when he had met her she had been a healthy weight but as the years went on, she lost her appetite for anything but vodka and cocaine, and when Pilot had left her, her addictions had only gotten worse. Now she looked to be under 100 pounds.

Of course, Genie herself didn't mind the weight loss at all. In her circle of Upper East Side friends, she was the thinnest, could fit into the sample sizes of all the best fashion designers, and reveled in her addictions. Apart from cocaine, Adderall, and the occasional speedball, she would start every day using meth. Her fragile, brittle blonde beauty was already beginning to crack at the seams. Pilot would have felt sorry for her but her cruelty made him feel numb to her downfall.

"My darling," she came toward him now and he couldn't help but back up a few paces. She noticed and anger flashed in her eyes, but she struggled and smiled. "Don't be scared of me, my darling. Pilot, after everything, the life we built, the love we had, don't you think we deserve more than this, this sad little divorce?"

"We've discussed this before, Genie, when you weren't high. We both know it's over. It has been for years. Maybe, it should never have even started."

Genie ignored him. "We never tried for children because of your career, and so now, I think it's time."

Oh God, she really was on one of her diatribes. Pilot rubbed his face. *How am I going to get her out of my apartment without her losing her shit on me—again?*

"Genie, I have a meeting I have to get to. Go home, sober up, and you'll realize the nonsense you're talking. We're divorced. No children. Not from me."

He took her shoulders and steered her out of the apartment, feeling how bony and frail her body felt. "Goodbye, Genie." The last he saw of her, her mouth was flapping uselessly, like a goldfish as she blinked in astonishment at her speedy banishment.

He shut the door quickly and leaned back against it. It wasn't that he was afraid of her—he was more afraid of the repercussions if she attacked him again. He was three times her weight and size—if he fought back and hurt her, he knew which side the police would come down on and it wouldn't be his. Plus, her family had connections. The Ratcliffe-Morgans were old money, not the 'nouveau riche' of men like his father, a self-made billionaire, and during their marriage, Eugenie had made it very cleared that his money was inferior. She hated that he made no attempt to battle the prenup, that he wasn't interested in money at all. It gave her one less thing to hold over him.

Now, his buzz from earlier destroyed, Pilot grabbed his bag and dug out the Polaroids, wanting to get back some of the excitement he had felt. He flicked through the photographs and found the ones of Boh. A warmth replaced the anxiety in his stomach. He snagged his phone from his jacket and sent her a message.

Really excited to be working with you, Boh. Pilot.

He hadn't expected her to reply so quickly and when he saw her message, he smiled.

You too! I've just been on the Internet to research some stuff —you are the king of Pinterest! Looking forward to starting work. B.

Sweet. Pilot glanced at the clock. Just after six p.m. He hesitated for a moment then typed in another message. Have you eaten yet?

Not yet, I just got out of rehearsal.

Pilot drew in a deep breath. Was this inappropriate? Ah, to hell with it.

Feel like grabbing a burger and getting started?

He counted the second before she replied. Sounds good. Where should I meet you?

Pilot couldn't help the victorious "Yes" that escaped his lips.

CHAPTER SIX

"The seasons."

"Been done."

"Um ... the elements?"

"Also done."

"Dang it." Boh shoved another bite of burger into her mouth and screwed up her face. Pilot grinned at her, a blob of mustard on the side of his own mouth. Without thinking, she reached over and swept it off with her finger. Immediately getting that it was a very intimate thing to do to someone she didn't know, she flushed, but Pilot just smiled and thanked her.

To cover her embarrassment, she made a joke of it. "I did contemplate leaving it there and letting you walk out of here, but I thought it was too early in our working relationship to do that."

Pilot laughed—God, his smile was intoxicating. "Well, I'm glad you thought so ... because now I can tell you about the ketchup on your cheek."

Boh's eyes widened, and she scrubbed furiously at both of her cheeks with the sleeve of her sweater. She checked but there was no ketchup on the fabric. Pilot gave her his best cheesy grin.

"Kidding."

Boh giggled. Over the last hour, she had learned that Pilot had the same goofy sense of humor that she did, and although she had been nervous when they first met up, now she was having a great time. They'd talked about the project and now Pilot had his notebook out in front of him.

"I thought we could just spitball ideas until we come up with a theme," he'd said after they'd ordered their food. They were at Bubby's on Hudson Street, and Boh was eating the most sublime burger she'd ever tasted, a mid-rare burger with fries. She'd skipped lunch—well, she'd been forced to skip lunch when Kristof made her make up for missing so much of his class—and now she was ravenous.

It didn't hurt that her view was so pleasant. Pilot, dressed in a dark navy sweater, his hair wild about his head, a dark five-o-clock shadow on his handsome face, was talking about themes and they were trying to think of something original.

"How about a ballerina in urban decay settings?"

Boh considered. "I do like that idea, but there's also a growing trend of urban ballet and I wonder if we could run into trouble there."

Pilot was tapping into his phone. "Yeah, you're right and of course, it's—"

"Already been done?"

Pilot chuckled. "Yep. Damn, I thought we had this."

Boh smiled shyly at him. "Come on, we've barely started. So, no elements, seasons, city dumps ..."

Pilot laughed. "And, please, God, no star signs."

"Amen to that." Boh stuck a French fry into her mouth. He was so easy to be with.

Pilot studied her. "What's Kristof's workshop about?"

"Sex and Death is the theme. He's pushing to do the murder

scene in The Lesson as part of the performance. Celine and Liz are fighting him."

"I don't know the ballet."

Boh leaned forward, in her element talking about her art, her passion. "The Lesson is the story of a teacher and his pupil. He's obsessed with her and during one particular lesson, he becomes more and more aroused by her performance until finally he snaps and stabs her to death."

Pilot grimaced. "Delightful."

Boh laughed. "Actually, when performed in the context of obsessive love, it is quite beautiful. The idea of being so in love with someone that you'd hurt them is something a lot of ballets cover. Mayerling, for example." She saw the strange look pass over his face. "What is it?"

He shook his head. "It's just ... the reality of that kind of relationship. There's nothing romantic about it."

She wondered who had hurt this beautiful man but didn't feel she could ask him directly. "Are you married, Pilot?"

"Divorced. Happily so."

Boh studied her fingernails. "Girlfriend?"

He didn't answer for a moment and she looked up to find him smiling at her, his eyes soft. "No, no girlfriend. You?"

She shook her head. Pilot leaned forward and gently brushed his lips against hers then drew back, his eyes searching hers. "Was that okay?"

Boh was having a hard job catching her breath. "More than okay," she whispered, and Pilot chuckled and kissed her again.

"You realize," he murmured against her lips, "that I'm just relieving you of ketchup and mustard. You have it all over your face."

They kissed again, and Boh's palms cupped her face, stroking the soft skin above his beard. *Ask me to come home with you* and I will, she silently asked him, shocking herself, but he made no attempt to try to talk her into his bed and she found herself warming to him. Yes, there was damage there, she thought, but Pilot Scamo was different to most men. She felt, in her bones, that he didn't want to take from her and that was new to her.

They talked some more but couldn't find an idea. "Let's call it a night," he said. "You look bushed. Can I drive you home?"

She got into his comfortable Mercedes and noted how worn it looked. Worn but comfortable, like an old friend. She knew nothing about cars, but the fact that he wasn't prissy about his made her smile. He saw her expression. "What?"

She told him and he laughed. "Yeah, she's just an old jalopy, really, but she's been very faithful to me."

"Can I ask you something?"

"Sure?"

"You come from money?"

Pilot nodded. "I can say that, yes, but there was a time before my dad made his money that I remember very well. Fifty-cent noodles from the bodega and cereal for dinner. My mom, she's a tenured professor at Columbia, but back then she was working her way up, plus bringing up a teenager and a baby, while Dad was working all hours at his company."

"What work did he do?"

"Really want to know?" Pilot gave her a grin, and she chuckled.

"As long as it's not gun-running."

"You might wish it was when I tell you."

Boh smiled. "Amaze me."

"Well," Pilot steered the car onto the Brooklyn Bridge, "You know those little perforations in toilet paper? My dad invented the perfect 'tear-rate'."

Boh blinked. That was the last thing she'd expected to hear. "Really?"

Pilot slid his eyes over to her. "Nope."

For a second Boh didn't comprehend what he'd said, then she busted out laughing. "You had me. You really had me."

Pilot chuckled. "Well, it was a more interesting line than he worked real hard in the city and made a wad of cash."

"You are quite insane, Pilot Scamo." She giggled, shaking her head.

They joked with each other on the way back to her apartment, then he walked her to her door. "Goodnight, Boheme Dali."

He kissed her gently, and she smiled. "Goodnight, Pilot. Thank you for dinner, for driving me home, and—thank you."

He stroked her cheek. "May I call you tomorrow?"

She nodded, and he kissed her one more time before he waved goodbye.

Boh went inside to find Grace asleep on the couch, Beelzebub curled on top of her head, awake, watching Boh with baleful eyes. "You're just jealous I got to kiss a gorgeous man," she whispered, draping a blanket over Grace's sleeping form.

When she was in bed, all she could think about was Pilot's kiss, his sweet smile, his touch, and she wished she were curled up next to him right now.

When she slept, she dreamed of dancing into his arms and never leaving that loving embrace. When she woke, she woke to a text message of two words.

Lightning bolt.

CHAPTER SEVEN

"I wasn't being cheesy, I swear, but it just came to me. I was thinking about meeting you, and then when I got home, some hokey rom-com movie was on cable. That one with the guy with the floppy hair, says fuck a lot."

Boh giggled. "Four Weddings and a Funeral?"

"That's the one." Pilot sipped his coffee. "Well, right at the very end, there's that meeting between the sick-kick guy and the posh woman, and there's this frisson. He even says it 'Gosh, thunderbolt city.' Are you laughing at my English accent?"

"No, no." Boh stuck her tongue in her cheek. Had she only known this man for 24 hours? Plot flicked a crumb of her bagel at her and she grinned. "So, carry on."

"Heard of Faraday cages?"

Boh screwed up her face. "Should I have?"

"Ah, the youth of today. Anyway, ignoramus, a Faraday cage is a kind of enclosure which will shield things, a human, anything from electricity. Say you got hit by lightning in your car —wouldn't hurt you because the car itself is a Faraday cage."

"Okay, I get that, Bill Nye, but what does it have to do with me, and our project?"

Pilot looked pleased with himself. "I'm glad you asked, Miss Sassy." He pulled out a sheet of paper on which he'd drawn something that resembled a birdcage. Inside of it, he'd drawn a figure, a ballerina, Boh, capturing her perfectly in mid-flight, her long limbs angled and graceful, mirroring the lightning bolts that were hitting the cage.

"Wow."

"You like it? The idea?"

"I like the idea and the sketch. How the hell did you catch my likeness so well?"

Pilot grinned. "It's a useful skill to have. But, seriously, what do you think? A series of movement and power. I'm not saying we do the entire shoot in a Faraday cage; I see it as a progression, maybe you in the cage at first, even hiding from the element until later in the series when you're almost battling with it. I'm rambling."

"You are, a little, but I think it's a great start." She looked back at the sketch. She loved the visual of it. "Would you do it as a modern piece or retro? Because I'm think this would look great as sepia-toned thing ... God, listen to me. You're the photographer."

Pilot leaned forward. "Listen, this is a collaboration, Boh. We work together. Besides ... you can order me around any time you like."

"Ha, don't say that," she laughed, blushing. Pilot traced a line with his fingertip across her palm and smiled at her.

"Will you be late for class?"

She shook her head. "I'm not scheduled until nine. I'm glad you called."

"Are you free for dinner later?"

She made a face. "That I don't know. Kristof is still running Vlad and me ragged and his usual trick is to keep us late on weeknights. Yesterday, I was lucky. May I let you know later?"

"Of course. Look, I have meetings in Manhattan all day so any time you have free to talk about the project, I'd appreciate it, but I also know you have to have downtime, so I won't be offended if you cry off."

Boh secretly thought that she would love to spend her downtime with Pilot, but she also knew she had to be mature about this. The last thing she wanted him to think was that she was a star-struck schoolgirl with a crush. He was studying her as if trying to read her mind.

"This has all happened quickly, and Boh, I want you to know —" he faltered and looked away, "I kissed you."

"Yes."

"That wasn't very professional of me, and I'm aware you might think it's something I always do with my subjects. You can believe me or not, but I don't. I haven't. I've never been a player, despite what my ex-wife might say. If any of this makes you uncomfortable, I want you to tell me."

He was letting her down, obviously regretting kissing her. Boh swallowed the lump in her throat and nodded.

"I appreciate that." She could feel her cheeks burning. Here, in front of her, was a world-famous photographer, and when she'd searched him on the Internet, she'd been disbelieving that the man who had kissed her and joked around with her could be so very out of her league. "I do have to focus on the performance," she said quietly, but managed to smile at him, "as well as our project."

"I would never put your job in jeopardy, Boh, I promise." He smiled at her. "Boh ... I'm twice your age, divorced, and a wreck. You deserve more."

Boh wondered that the atmosphere between them had changed so suddenly from fun-loving to serious. "Pilot, I'm not someone who craves other people's company, in fact, I actively seek out situations where I can be alone. But I like spending time with you."

Pilot smiled. "Same here. Friends?"

"Friends."

PILOT WALKED Boh back to the ballet company and then bid her goodbye. As he walked back to the car, he shook his head. He'd stayed awake all night thinking about her and the usual doubts about his self-worth had come flooding in. He'd tried to argue that he shouldn't ignore the kind of chemistry that had been instantly there between them, but neither could he bring Boh into his shitty life at the moment. Once he was free of Eugenie, maybe.

So he'd given Boh an out.

Damn it.

His phone buzzed, and he saw it was his mother calling. "Hey, Mom."

"Hey, cutie. How are you? I haven't heard from you for a few days."

Pilot smiled to himself. Since his divorce, Blair Scamo had been more attentive than usual, worried that her son would fall into one of the depressive moods he was prone to. Blair had disliked Eugenie from the beginning, but she also respected her son's decisions and had been polite and kind to Eugenie throughout the marriage. She'd also seen Pilot at his most broken, when Eugenie's cruelty had taken his pride, his confidence, and on more than one occasion, his health.

"I'm ..." He was about to tell her that he was good, but he knew it would be a lie. Eugenie's latest visit had put a strain on him that he was finding hard to get past. He sighed. "Genie came to see me the other day. She wants a baby."

"Oh, for the love of God." He could hear his mother's anger. "I've said it before, Pilot. You need to ghost her, cut her out entirely."

He was silent for a moment, and when Blair spoke again, her tone was softer. "Sometimes I forget the man I raised. You're too good, Pilot, and I know that sounds strange. You were a victim of domestic abuse, Pilot—"

"Don't say that, Mom, please." Pilot winced at his mother's words.

"Don't be a macho man. There's no shame in admitting that, Pilot. It happens to the strongest people, the very strongest. The strong and the good. It's time, my boy."

THE TROUBLE WAS—PILOT was embarrassed. Humiliated on more than one occasion by Genie in public, physically and emotionally attacked in private. Subconsciously, he touched the half-moon scar at the corner of his right eye. A broken champagne bottle that time. It could have ended his career, and he had no doubt that was exactly what Genie had wanted—to hurt him in the worst way.

He knew what he had to do. A new apartment, try to keep the details out of the press. He should keep the one in his present building as a decoy. It was a start.

That was the other reason he had backed away from Boh. Eugenie's jealousy knew no limits and if she found out he was seeing someone else—someone so much younger and, in Pilot's opinion, far more beautiful and sweet—he couldn't bear the thought of Boh getting caught up in the ferocity of Genie's rage.

God, what a fucking mess of a life. He could feel the black cloud descending on him. He stopped and got his bearings. What was next? What was he on his way to do?

He checked his schedule on his phone and turned down Broadway, making his way to his studio.

Work. Work was what would push the pain away, although he wished with all his being that when he reached his studio, Boh would be there to hold him in her arms.

CHAPTER EIGHT

"Where the fuck have you been?"

Kristof's rage filled the studio, and, humiliated, Boh put her bag down before she answered him, trying to keep her voice steady. "I wasn't scheduled until nine, Kristof, and it's ten of now."

She saw Serena smirk. Kristof's dark eyes burrowed into hers. "So we're adding illiterate to tardy now?" He stormed outside of the studio and Boh saw him rip the class schedules from the corkboard on the wall outside the studio. Her heart sank. Clearly, there had been another late schedule change. Kristof came in and shoved the piece of paper at her. Sure enough, under her name was "Mendelev, Studio 6, 8 a.m."

"I didn't see this. When I left last night, it was still—"

"I don't want your fucking excuses, Boh. Get changed into the white leotard."

Ah. He often made them change into different clothes to better see the lines of their bodies when they danced. She grabbed her bag and headed out of the door.

"No. Get changed—here."

Boh stopped, shocked. A murmur went around the class.

What the hell? Kristof's eyes gleamed with malice. "Do it. Clearly, you don't mind stripping down for Pilot Scamo, so, so shy?"

"What the hell are you talking about?"

"You're fucking him. We all know about it. So, come on. Get changed and let us all see what he sees."

Serena gave a chuckle and Boh shot her a fierce glare. "Who I see in my private time is my business, but you're wrong. Pilot Scamo and I are just friends and I have no intention of stripping off just because you're in one of your petty tempers, Kristof."

Boh heard the gasp from some of her cohort, and she was shocked at her own response to the man. She saw anger ripple across his face. "Strip or get out," he said steadily. "And someone else will dance the lead in the workshop."

Bastard. She would not let him take what she had worked so hard for. Pulling her arms into her sweatshirt, she yanked the bottom of it down to cover her ass and stripped off her pants and underwear. Kristof watched her in amusement as she deftly changed into her leotard without exposing any intimate parts.

"There, that wasn't so hard, was it? Now, first positions."

Boh was still angry at the end of the class, and they all walked back to the changing rooms, she hooked her finger in the back of Serena's top and yanked her back. "Keep your filthy little rumors to yourself, bitch."

Serena extracted herself from Boh's grip and gave her the finger. "We're all pretty sick of this precious little virgin routine, Dali. No one believes it. So fuck you and your skeevy photographer."

Boh, incensed, lunged for the other girl, but Grace and Fernanda pulled her back. "Fuck off, Serena," Grace said, and, snickering, Serena walked away. "Ignore her, Boh, she's just being—"

"A little cu—"

"Boh! This isn't like you. Come on." Grace hauled her away, down to the cafeteria. When they were seated, Boh sighed and folded her arms on the table, resting her head on them.

"Sorry, Gracie," she said, "I'm a grouch today."

Gracie studied her. "You were already gone when I left the apartment this morning. Where did you go?"

Boh could feel her face burn. "I had a breakfast meeting with Pilot Scamo."

Grace smiled. "You like him."

"I do, but this is a working relationship." He'd made that clear, she thought sadly. She tried to smile at Grace. "But he's going to be working with all of us, and so I would hate for any rumors to get back to him, embarrass him. Untrue rumors."

"You're sweet, but I think Scamo can look after himself. He is a phenomenal photographer." Grace was flicking through some of Pilot's images on her phone. She smiled at her friend. "If anyone can capture you, Boh, it's him. I can't wait to see what he does."

"With all of us," Boh corrected but couldn't help the little smile that escaped from her. Grace laughed and squeezed her arm.

"You know what, Boh? If you have a crush, that's okay. You can date who you want. You should date, at your age. How come you never have?"

Boh felt the usual dread seep into her chest, the fear that always followed when someone questioned her solitary life. But before she could answer her, their attention was caught by the elderly woman walking slowly into the room, her gaze wheeling around, her expression one of confusion. Grace and Boh were up immediately to go to her side.

"Madam Vasquez? Are you okay?"

The elderly woman smiled at them both. "June, Sally, how lovely to see you."

Grace and Boh exchanged a glance. Eleonor Vasquez was a former prima ballerina, one of the world's greatest, with one of the longest careers of a dancer ever, her career mercifully unhampered by serious injury. What ended her career eventually was the scandal of her lifelong love affair with Celine Peletier becoming public in an age when homosexuality and lesbian relationship were still taboo.

Vasquez, a firebrand from Argentina, had made a public statement about her love for the Frenchwoman. "My dancing career was my passion," she told reporters, "but my love Celine is my life."

The two women had been together for over 50 years now, but time had caught up with Eleonor a decade ago. Dementia. The ballet company, loyal to her to the last, allowed her to live with Celine in one of the company's apartments next to the studios, and even allowed her to "teach" still. A few of the dancers would give the extra time to be taught by this living legend, Boh and Grace among them. They didn't mind being whoever she wanted them to be for that hour.

Serena and some of the others wouldn't give that time, dismissing the elderly woman as a "demented fool." But the love Eleonor and Celine shared was an inspiration to most of the troupe, and their support, Boh knew, meant the world to Celine Peletier.

She and Grace walked Eleonor back to her apartment now, where they were met by an exasperated looking Celine. "You wandered off again?"

Eleonor beamed at her lover. "How lovely to see you, Petal," she said, using her pet names for Celine. Celine rolled her eyes and steered Eleonor into the apartment. She smiled gratefully at Boh and Grace. "Thank you, girls. Now, my little white swan, let's get you to bed."

Grace closed the door quietly and the two women walked slowly back down to the studios.

"Puts any little annoyance into perspective, doesn't it?"

Boh nodded. "It does." She recalled the way Eleonor and Celine looked at each other and her heart ached. To have so much love and to risk losing your partner to the relentless horror of dementia ... she couldn't imagine. Their love made her crush on Pilot seem even more ridiculous. He was a grownup and she was just a kid ... no matter if their attraction had been so palpable it was insane.

"What's on your mind?" Grace asked her, but Boh just nodded.

"Nothing. Let's go dance."

SERENA SNORTED the ivory white line from the table and wiped her nostrils, grinning at Kristof as she laid back on top of him. "That was a particularly cruel trick you played on little Miss Perfect this morning, but I have to say, I enjoyed it."

She straddled his naked form and reached for his cock, stroking it, trying to get him hard again. He was smoking a joint, watching her carefully. She knew this look in his eyes; it was spite. His cock remained limp, and she gave up, rolling onto the side of his bed and getting up.

"Where are you going?"

"To pee."

She went into the bathroom and sat down on the toilet. Sex with Kristof had been thrilling at the start. The first day she had arrived at the company, already an established member of another rival company, he had singled her out, asked her to stay after the final class of the day.

He'd fucked her in his office, bending her over his desk and thrusting hard. Since then, two years ago, they'd continued to screw each other but Serena had been disappointed that it had gotten her no further than soloist. She'd begged Kristof to make her principal after the former lead had moved on, and she had thought she was close to it. But then Kristof had seen Boheme Dali dance and promoted her to principal instead.

He'd pacified a furious Serena with even more sex, and as many appetite-suppressing drugs and cocaine as she could handle, but still, it rankled. Serena knew Boh was the superior dancer—hell, Serena secretly loved to watch the other girl dance—but her upbringing meant she expected nothing to be denied to her. So she made Boh's life a misery.

And she knew something about Boheme that no one else did. Crashing a party at Boh and Grace's apartment, she'd seen a handwritten letter addressed to Boh and had pocketed it on a whim. She hadn't imagined the contents of that letter would be so salacious, so useful. Boh's daddy was a bad, bad man. Boh's pure virginal act was just that, an act, even if she was the victim of her pedophile father. Serena had kept Boh's secret, not out of charity, but she was waiting for the opportune moment to drop it on her.

Maybe that moment was coming sooner than later, Serena pondered now as she washed her hands. She toyed with telling Kristof about the letter but decided against it. Her erstwhile lover was already too damn preoccupied with Boh as it was. She looked in the mirror, seeing her strawberry blonde hair was messy and was sticking to the sweat on her forehead. She splashed water on her face and smoothed down her hair. As she walked back in the bed, Kristof was scribbling in his notebook, working out choreography, she knew.

She laid back beside him on the bed. "Finally decided on the playlist yet?"

Kristof nodded. "We're doing The Lesson whether Liz likes it or not. It's the perfect ballet for a sex and death theme. Darkness, obsession. For Chrissake, Nureyev danced it, so I don't understand Liz's reticence."

"I think she's worried about the violence against woman thing in these days of Me Too," Serena said dryly. She selected a ready rolled joint from Kristof's silver cigarette case and lit it, coughing immediately and grimacing. She'd never liked pot. It made her goofy, whereas the coke gave her superhuman energy. Kristof looked annoyed and snatched the joint from her.

"Don't waste it. This is top market shit."

Serena looked at him slyly. "Who are you getting clean pee from? I know you must be getting it from someone, one of the guys. Who owes you a favor like that, Kristof?"

His eyes glinted dangerously and Serena felt a frisson of fear shoot through her. That Kristof was mercurial was well-known but at that moment, Serena saw something else in his eyes and the word that shot into her brain was ... unhinged. Shit.

"Never mind." She reached for his cock again and this time, she did get him hard. She straddled him, gently taking his notebook from him and running her hands over his chest as she slowly impaled herself on his cock.

Kristof's expression changed from annoyance to satisfaction as they began to fuck again and as Serena moved on top of him, he grabbed her hair and fisted it in his hands, crushing his mouth against hers then groaning, "Oona ... Oona ... I'm sorry, I'm sorry ..."

Serena waited until after he had fallen asleep to cry.

CHAPTER NINE

"Again."

Boh gritted her teeth and return to her first position. The combination was difficult, but she knew she had it down. Kristof was just being an ass. Whether he knew she was supposed to be meeting with Pilot right now, she didn't know, but the fact that she was there alone after Vlad and Jeremy had already left made her think he did. She danced the combination twice more for him, each time step-perfect.

Kristof sighed as she finished in arabesque. "Again."

"Not again," Liz Secretariat walked into the room, giving Boh a smile. "Even from the corridor I could see you were perfect, Boh. Kristof, we need to talk, Boh, you can go."

"And who the hell are you to ... oh, what the hell." Kristof gave a long-suffering sigh. "Get lost," he snapped at Boh, who managed to give him the finger behind his back. Liz hid a smile and winked at Boh as she left.

Boh ran to the changing room, half-undressing even before she got there. Boh hurriedly showered and changed into a wrap-around dress over another clean leotard. She and Pilot were shooting test shots today, working out the movements she would perform for him.

She ran through the rainy city streets on Manhattan, her excitement about seeing him again making her breathless and almost giddy.

He was waiting for her at his studio and kissed her cheek as she came into the room. "You're soaking wet."

Boh shrugged but allowed him to take off her coat and wrap her in a towel. "Come and get warm. I have coffee."

She sat, swaddled in his huge towel, sipping coffee as he ran her through some ideas. "To be honest, the steps all have to come from you ... I have ideas about shapes I would like you to translate into dance, if you could?"

Boh nodded, loving to see Pilot in full creative mode. "I'd love to." She looked at the floor of the studio. Brushed wooden boards, which hopefully had a little give. He saw her looking at them and smiled.

"I admit ... I had the floor redone especially for you, as best as I could. Come test it for me."

Boh slipped into her ballet shoes to begin with and slipped off her sweatshirt. She wore nothing but her leotard and a small skirt around her waist. She saw Pilot's eyes drop to her nipples, cold from the weather, poking through the thin material, then look away quickly, and smiled. She longed for him to touch her and fantasized about grabbing his hand and pressing it to her chest, or between her legs, but forced herself to focus.

She walked over to where he had set up the camera and stood in front of it. "Should I just freestyle?"

"Whatever feels natural, baby."

Baby. A shiver of pleasure tingled down her spine. She began with small but delicate moves, then bolder jetés and pirouettes.

"Imagine you're fighting lightning," Pilot suggested, his eyes locked on her through the camera, "or that you are lightning."

"Maybe a little music would help." She ran to her bag and pulled out her MP3 player. Pilot plugged it into his stereo for her and she flicked through the playlists until she found the song she wanted. Immediately "Raise Hell," by Dorothy boomed through the studio and Pilot grinned.

"Good choice."

Inspired by the rock music, Boh let loose and jumped and whirled for him, sometimes, grinning, sometimes with a fierce look of determination on her face. Pilot clicked away, shouting encouragement over the music, occasionally stopping to drag props into the frame, things like an old paint-spattered crate for her to pose on top of, or a heavy old rope to wind around her frame.

"Holy shit, Boh," he said as she paused to catch her breath, "you belong in front of a camera. Some of these are good enough to be in the show and we're just getting started."

"I think that's because of you, Pilot, not me," she was slightly breathless, but laughing. She came to see some the shots and gave a little gasp. "Is that really me?"

Pilot chuckled. "It really is. See what I mean? You're a goddess."

They were standing close, very close, Boh's left breast against his chest as she leaned over him to look in his camera. She looked up into his eyes and their gazes locked. For a long moment, they stared at each other, then Pilot gave a small smile.

"We could slow things down now, do some more fluid movements."

Her heart beating fast, she willed herself to move away from him. "I've been working on something," she told him, a little nervousness creeping into her voice. "No one's seen it yet, but if you'd like to?"

"I'd be honored."

Trembling, Boh changed the music on the stereo. "You know Olafur Arnalds?"

"The Icelandic composer? I do."

She smiled, pleased. "He has this song, "Reminiscence" that I love and as soon as I heard it, I wanted to dance to it. It's very rough but—"

She began to move to the music, using a combination of ballet and freestyle dancing to twist and curve her into shapes to the somber, delicate music, pouring all of her emotions into the dance, closing her eyes, letting all of her pain at her family, her love for her art, and her hidden sensuality flow through her. She heard the click of Pilot's camera at first but when it stopped, she opened her eyes and saw him.

He was no longer taking shots, but watching her, his green eyes full of ... what? She continued the dance but kept returning to his gaze, dancing for him now alone, letting her attraction to him radiate through her body, a yearning, a need.

As the music came to a close, she stepped to him, drawing her fingertips down his cheek. She heard his ragged breathing and smiled. Very slowly and deliberately, she pulled the shoulder of her leotard down and exposed her naked breast. For a moment, she thought he might pull away, then with a groan, he bent his head and his mouth closed around her nipple.

Boh swayed a little, not expecting the rush of pleasure that flooded her system. She tangled her fingers in his curls as his tongue flicked around the nipple, and his mouth sucked hungrily at her. His arms snaked around her waist and pulled her against him and she could feel his cock, thick and long against his blue jeans, and how much he wanted her.

He looked up, and she nodded at the question in his eyes. Her body was screaming for his touch. His hands went to the bun of her hair and released it so it flowed down her back.

"Boh ... are you sure?"

She nodded again, not trusting herself to speak in case she broke the spell. Pilot swept her up unto his arms and carried her to the couch against the far wall of the studio. She let her head drop onto his shoulder, her lips against his neck, and when he laid her down, he covered her body with his. He swept the hair away from her face, his eyes full of desire.

She kissed him, her mouth seeking his lips as her hands went under his T-shirt to stroke his stomach, the muscles hard and quivering under her touch. Pilot reached over his head and pulled his T-shirt off in one easy motion.

Boh sighed at the broad shoulders, hard pecs, and traced the small tattoo on his arm. "What is it?"

"Sorry to be prosaic," he grinned, kissing her throat, "but it's just the family crest."

"No, I like it." She was trembling now as he gently peeled her leotard down, exposing both her breasts and her belly. He bent down to kiss the soft curve of it, his tongue rimming around her navel.

"Christ, you're beautiful," he murmured as slowly, his fingers worked around to the fastening on her skirt."

Then they both froze as someone banged on the studio door. "Pilot!"

"Fuck." Pilot rolled off Boh and tugged his shirt on. He handed Boheme her sweatshirt. "I'm sorry, baby. I'll get rid of her."

He darted to the door and pulled it open. Boh was shell-shocked, but she slid into her sweatshirt and pretended to be tying her ballet shoe ribbons.

"Eugenie ... what the hell are you doing here?" Pilot sounded pissed—and exhausted.

A pin-thin blonde woman pushed past him. "You were supposed to call me back, Pilot. I left messages. What—" She stopped when she saw Boh. Boh stared back at the other woman, keeping her face bland.

"Hello," she said politely. The blonde woman—Eugenie—stared back at her.

"And who the hell is this?"

"Not," Pilot said with a voice like ice, "that it's any of your business, but this is Boh. She's posing for me for my exhibition. Boh is a principal with the NYSMBC. I know you've heard of them—didn't you fuck Wally after their last benefit?"

Boh winced but Eugenie ignored the jibe. She walked to inspect Boh more closely. Boh stood her ground but she could smell liquor on the other woman's breath, see the faint dusting of coke on her upper lip.

Eugenie looked her up and down. "You are the principal?"

"Yes." Boh kept her tone even, neither friendly nor rude.

Eugenie smirked. "Are you even American?"

"Okay, that's it." Pilot grabbed Eugenie by her upper arm and steered her towards the door. Eugenie cackled. "She tells you she's the principal, Pilot, but I suspect she's just the help ..."

Pilot, his face creased in anger, pushed her out of the door and slammed it. He turned to Boh, who was standing, shocked. Had that just happened? Had that scrawny bitch really called her the help? Boh had suffered enough racism in her life that she had come to expect it, but so out of the blue like that?

"Boh, I'm so sorry, I—"

"Who the fuck was that?" She looked at him with disbelieving eyes.

Pilot's shoulders slumped. "My ex-wife."

"You were married to that?" Boh realized her voice was getting higher, but the shock of almost sleeping with him, then being interrupted by that ...

Pilot nodded and she noticed how tired he looked, how

distressed. Her face softened and she went to him, wrapping her arms around him. "It's okay."

He buried his face in her shoulder. "It's not," his voice was muffled, "but it's my reality." He looked up, and Boh was shocked by the pain in his eyes. "I'm so sorry, Boh."

"It's not your fault." She placed her palm against his cheek. He leaned into her touch and she stroked her thumb over his face. "What did she do to you?" Her voice was a whisper.

Pilot shook his head. "I really don't want to talk about it, if you don't mind."

"I don't mind." She gave him a small smile. "We're not at the sharing histories part yet."

Plot smiled at her. "And, although there's nothing more I'd like than to make love to you, Boh ... we're not there yet either. I'm sorry about earlier."

She wasn't stung; she knew he was right. "I know. Call that ... second base."

He chuckled. "I want to do this right," he told her, his eyes serious. "Let's work together, and date. Have fun before it gets too ... everything is so fast these days. What about anticipation? What about slow burn?" He pressed his lips to hers. "And there's so much to consider if we decide to give it a go. But, for now, what I'd like, what I so desperately need, Boh, is fun."

She chuckled. "Then you've got it, handsome." She sighed. "But I think I should go, now."

He smiled. "Please stay. We can order pizza, watch old movies, talk about the pictures we took."

Boh weighed how she was feeling. Her emotions were still roiling around inside her, her desire for Pilot overwhelming, but the mood had been ruined by his vicious ex-wife. Did she really want her first time with him to be sullied by that?

No.

But she also didn't want to say goodbye. She touched his

face. "I'd liked that." She was rewarded by the boyish grin she loved. They settled on the couch when their food arrived, then watched movies and talked late into the night. They fell asleep on the couch, arms wrapped around each other. As Boh gave into unconsciousness, she smiled as she felt Pilot's lips against hers and wished she could fall asleep this way for the rest of her life.

10

CHAPTER TEN

Kristof was celebrating. After Boh had left, he and Liz had finally sat down to discuss his show. "The Lesson," he said firmly, and raised his hands before she could argue with him. "Non-negotiable. You know my reasons—it's the ultimate sex and death ballet."

Liz sighed. "And the most controversial." She contemplated for a moment then turned back to him. "All right. I'll agree on condition we include, in the other two parts, ballets with a softer side to them. Romeo and Juliet, and La Sylphide."

Kristof nodded. "Fine. La Sylphide first, then Romeo, then The Lesson as the finale." He remembered a promise. "Boh and Vlad for La Sylphide, Serena and Jeremy for Romeo, then Boh and Elliott for The Lesson. That's who I want, Liz."

"You're promoting Serena to principal?"

"Hell, no. Soloist, but I need a different face for Romeo."

Liz studied him. "Boh's ready?"

"More than, despite what I tell her. Never hurts to keep them guessing." Kristof sighed, absentmindedly rubbing his nose. Liz never missed a thing.

"You'll remember to submit your urine sample for testing?"

Kristof gave her a supercilious smile. "Every Friday lunchtime, like clockwork. Don't worry, Liz. I know what I have to do to keep my job."

Now, as he took a cab home to his apartment in Lenox Hill, Kristof smiled to himself. Whether or not he took drugs wouldn't matter after the showcase. His work would be seen, once again, as ground-breaking, visceral, dramatic, and with Boh as the focus, the first Indian American principal ... the sky was the limit.

He opened the door of the apartment and kicked a pile of mail into the corner. He didn't even glance at it, knowing what the brown envelopes meant. He'd wait until the ones with the red 'Urgent' mark arrived. He had better things to worry about.

Now that he'd gotten the green light, he wanted to move things along. He'd set up rehearsals, and the dancers would have to suck up the long hours. They needed to be beyond perfect.

He smiled and sat down at his desk, grabbing fresh paper and pencils. Before the end of the week he would have it, the outline, ready to work with the dancers on the choreography.

For once, Kristof didn't snort his way into oblivion. He needed his mind sharp. As he wrote and drew steps and costumes, he pictured his Boh as the Pupil in The Lesson, cowed and terrified as the Teacher approached her with his knife.

Boh woke and smiled as she saw Pilot asleep next to her. She watched him, his long dark eyelashes on his cheeks, his beard longer now. She gently traced the dark violet circles under his eyes, and he opened them, their brilliant green always startling to her.

"Good morning."

He smiled and pressed his lips to hers. "Good morning, beautiful. Sorry about the morning breath."

"Me too." But they kissed anyway. "I like waking up with you, Pilot."

He grinned and as they sat up and stretched, he drew her close and hugged her tightly. "Would you believe me if I said I slept better last night on this old lumpy couch than I have done in years, maybe a decade?"

"Same. Would it be cheesy to say that it was the best night of my life?" Boh smoothed his dark curls away from his face. "Okay, that was cheesy, but it's still true. You make me feel so safe, Pilot, so ... cared for."

He smiled. "So ... loved?"

Her heart skipped a beat. "What?"

He chuckled. "I'm not saying anything too over-the-top but we have something remarkable here between us, I think. I've never felt this ..." He cast around for the right word, then looked back at her. "This is right, you know? My gut tells me, everything tells me, we were meant to meet."

"I feel it," she said simply, "I feel that too." She leaned her forehead against his. "And ... thank you. Thank you for last night for before ... her and after. Most men would have taken what they wanted from me regardless of my feelings."

Pilot kissed her again, his lips tender against hers. "I'm not most men."

"You can say that again." Her eyes slid to the clock on the wall of the studio. "Dang it. I have to be at work in thirty minutes."

"There's a shower here in the little bathroom over there." He grinned. "I'd join you, but I don't think you'd make it to work in a half hour if I did."

Boh laughed. "I'd say that's a given."

When she'd finished in the bathroom—luckily, she always

carried changes of underwear with her for work—she found Pilot had made her a flask of coffee to have on the go. "I haven't got any cereal or bread here, but here." He gave her an energy bar and she smiled.

"Breakfast of champions."

"Do you want me to walk you to the studio?"

She shook her head. "You have work to do, baby." She flushed a little at the epithet which came out of her unbidden but his answering smile was worth it.

He kissed her goodbye at the door. "I'll call you later."

"Can't wait."

As she walked to work, sipping the coffee he had made for her, Boh felt like last night had been a dream. She had been telling him the truth when she told him she felt safe—to be that close to a man had always been traumatizing, if the other man hadn't been a ballet dancer—but with him …

Boh wondered how her gentle, kind, sweet-hearted Pilot could ever have been married to that blonde racist. Boh's face must have registered a scowl as a woman standing next to her at a crosswalk looked alarmed and edged away. Boh shot her an apologetic smile, then as they crossed, she thought about Pilot's ex again. When she'd Googled him, it had mentioned that his ex-wife was an Upper East Side woman who regularly did work for charity. There was nothing charitable about the woman she'd met last night.

"Oo, serious face. Who yanked your chain?" She hadn't seen Elliott falling in step beside her as they approached the NYSMBC building. She grinned at him. Elliott was one of her favorite people and he was an exquisite dancer.

"Ah, no one important. I feel like I haven't talked to you in an age, El."

"Right back at ya, sweet cheeks. But, I have news. Jeremy texted me earlier—Kristof's got clearance to do The Lesson."

Boh's eyebrows shot up. "Really? I thought Liz was going hard on him to drop it."

"He got it through. Although, she did make him include Romeo and Juliet—don't make that face, some of us like it." Elliott grinned at her grimace. "Although I don't hope to get one of the leads. Jeremy and Vlad will get them."

Boh studied her friend. "Still crushing hard on Jeremy?"

"I think I'm actually getting somewhere. We hung out the other night, just drinking and eating pizza, but it was good."

"Any action?" Boh smiled at him but inside she was annoyed. She knew Jeremy made the most of Elliott's crush on him, and she also didn't believe for a second that Jeremy had any intention of "being" with Elliott. He was using him and it pissed her off. But she couldn't interfere—it wasn't her place to. She just hoped Elliott wouldn't get hurt.

"Nah, but, you know, slow burn."

Boh smiled, remembering what Pilot had said last night. "I do know."

Elliott nudged her with his shoulder. "How come you dislike R and J so much?"

Because my father loves it. "It's that whole teen angst angle. I mean, your families are rich, and you're only a few years away from maturity when you can be together. Why kill yourselves, douchebags?"

Elliott snickered. "You don't believe in love at first sight?"

She was ready to say no, her usual answer, but now she didn't know if it was true. With how she felt about Pilot, from that first day—was it really any different from the insta-love between Shakespeare's teen lovers?

She pushed the thought away. I am not in love with Pilot

Scamo. Not yet. As they made their way into the building and to the changing rooms, they heard Serena's high, grating voice.

"I mean, why? Why does she get the spotlight shined on her? What's so fucking special about her?"

Boh and Elliott looked at each other and both rolled their eyes. Serena could only be bitching about Boh ... again.

"Boh is the principal whether you like it or not, Serena," Grace was saying as Boh and Elliott made their way into the changing room. Grace winked at Boh, who grinned back at her. Grace looked back at Serena. "Just be grateful you got the lead in the middle segment."

Boh raised her eyebrows at her friend and Grace smiled. "You're the lead for La Sylphide and The Lesson, babe. Congrats. No one could do a better job."

"Thanks, Gracie."

"Holy crap," Elliott was holding a piece of paper. He looked up, amazement in his eyes. "I'm your partner for The Lesson."

Boh was delighted for her friend. He had been toiling away in the corps de ballet for years, losing out to Vlad and Jeremy on leading roles most times. When Vlad had been promoted to principal danseur over Elliott, he had been crushed. Now he was overwhelmed and picked Boh up and spun her around.

Everyone except Serena laughed at them. She slammed down her makeup and stormed out of the room. "Ding dong, the witch is dead," Vlad sang in his Russian accent.

Their good mood lasted until Kristof's class, which had been extended to three hours, late in the afternoon. He ran them ragged, criticizing every plie or port des bras. "You look like a bunch of fucking construction workers," he spat at them.

Elliott started to sing "YMCA" and the others giggled. Kristof rounded on them, and they shut up. His small eyes focused on Elliott. "You think this is funny?"

Elliott shut his mouth, but Boh noticed a small smirk

playing around his lips. He met Kristof's eye and something passed between them she didn't understand.

Kristof huffed out a sigh but moved on. Huh. His usual trick of exploding and making an example of someone was missing today, and it freaked her out.

BY THE END of the day, Boh was exhausted. Kristof made her go over and over her choreography for La Sylphide, and now, when she took her shoes off, her toes were split and bleeding. She hoped Pilot didn't have a thing for feet because, any ballerina would tell you, their feet only looked beautiful in shoes while they danced.

"Ugh," she said, and wincing, tore off a loose piece of toenail. It could have been worse, but what was worse was the dizziness.

It had started around four in the afternoon and although Boh pushed through, it had gotten worse incrementally over time. She glanced at the clock. Seven p.m. She waited until the changing room emptied out then leaned her head against the cool tile wall and closed her eyes. Bright sparks flashed behind her eyelids and she felt as if she might throw up.

Her phone bleeped. *You done? Want me to come pick you up? P x*

Before she could answer, Grace came to find her and taking one look at her friend, knelt down beside her. "Hey, kiddo ... you dizzy again?"

"Again?"

Grace smiled softly at her. "The throwing up, the extra-strength iron tablets on your nightstand? We live together, Boh." She gently pulled the skin under Boh's eye down. "Anemia?"

Boh nodded. She should have guessed Grace would find out—she missed nothing.

Grace frowned at her. "How long?"

"A few months. It's mild, but sometimes ..."

"Yeah. Come on. I'll feed you raw steak and spinach, Popeye."

She helped Boh to her feet, but Boh hesitated and Grace suddenly smiled. "Unless you have a better offer?"

"Not a better offer," Boh protested, not wanting to hurt her friend's feelings, but Grace laughed.

"He's a sweetheart, that's what I hear," she said, lowering her voice. "Nelly was singing his praises when I was in her office the other day. Bitch of an ex-wife."

Boh chuckled. "Yes, I met her last night. She deserves that title."

"You stayed at his place?"

"His studio, on the couch." Boh could feel her face flame red, but she also couldn't hide her smile and Grace chuckled.

"You ready?"

Boh blinked. "For what?"

Grace's smile was wide. "For the first—and hopefully last—love of your life?"

EVEN THE SIGHT OF HER, hair mussed up, no makeup, was like a shot of pure heroin in Pilot's veins—not that he would know what that felt like—but he couldn't imagine it would be any better than Boh smiling at him. "Hey, beautiful girl."

"Hey, handsome."

He pushed himself away from his car where he'd been leaning and took her in his arms. Boh kissed him, but when she drew away, she swayed a little and he caught her. "You okay?"

"I'm a little dizzy, is all."

He tucked her into the passenger seat of the car. "Do you need a doctor?"

She smiled at him. "No, I'm fine. Just exhausted."

Pilot reached out and stroked her face tenderly. "Wanna come home with me? I can cook."

"You can?"

"Half-Italian, remember?" He grinned as she chuckled, hearing her sigh of happiness. He brushed his lips against hers, then, out of the corner, he saw Kristof, standing outside the building, watching them. Pilot drew away from Boh and gave Kristof a sarcastic salute.

Boh looked around and groaned. "Quick, drive, before he decides I need to rehearse for another three hours."

"I'd talk him out of it," Pilot said, his voice even. He saw Kristof finish his cigarette and step toward the car. Nope, asshole. She's tired, and she's coming home with me. Tempted to give Kristof the finger, he held back and instead pulled the car away from the curb.

By the time they got back to his apartment, Boh was asleep. Gently lifting her from the car, he carried her to the elevator and into his apartment.

He hesitated before taking her into his bedroom and laying her on the bed, pulling a blanket over her sleeping form, and easing her sneakers off of her feet.

He left her to sleep and went to the kitchen to prepare something for them to eat. His father had been a gastronome, a fact that probably contributed to his early heart attack at 56, but Pilot and his sister Ramona had both spent hours with him in their huge kitchens in their farmhouse in Italy and their mansion in New York State, learning the craft of cookery.

He made gnocchi now, from scratch, rolling the dough as his father taught him. *Pa, you would have been proud—and you would have loved Boh.* After he'd formed the tiny dough balls, he covered them with a damp cloth to await cooking when Boh woke up.

While he waited, he logged onto his laptop and went

through the shots they had done the previous day. Some of them were good enough to be in the exhibition in his opinion, and he'd sent a few test shots to Grady for his opinion. The answer came back straight away and confirmed what he, Pilot, had been contemplating all day. From Grady, it had been straight to the point. *This girl. No gimmicks. No theme. Just her.*

Pilot couldn't have agreed more. While he still loved the idea of the Faraday cages, that could wait until they had time to do it. Grady was right. This one was just Boh.

"Hey."

He looked up and saw her, leaning shyly against the door to the kitchen. He went to her and drew her into his arms. "Hey. Did you sleep okay?"

She nodded. "Sorry for nodding off on you."

He kissed her. "Never apologize. You were tired. You hungry?"

She nodded, and he took her hand. "Come watch me cook."

She sat with a glass of red wine in front of her, watching as Pilot prepared their supper. "You made this? All of it?"

Pilot grinned. "Told you I could cook."

"Is there anything you can't do?" There was no double meaning in her words and she was looking at him with eyes filled with nothing but ... love. He cleared his throat and looked away. The ego in him wanted her to believe he was perfect, but that was no way to start a relationship. "There's plenty I can't do, Boh. Plenty. I can't fix the mistakes I've made in my life."

"No one can, baby."

"I—" he faltered. "I made one big mistake, Boh, and even though I'm so happy with you, that mistake is still—"

"Eugenie?"

Pilot nodded. "For a man like me, for any man, to admit he's been abused by a domestic partner ... it's hard. But I cannot start this thing with you without you knowing what I've had to deal with, in case ... it comes back to hurt us. You're 22 years old, Boh and—"

"My father sexually assaulted me from the age of twelve," Boh interrupted him, her voice shaking. "My mother knew. My sisters knew. He died recently, and I refused to go to the funeral. My sister called me a whore. A whore." She got up and went to him. "And until the day I met you, I never knew what happiness could be. What trust and love and honesty meant. And until last night, the person I most wanted to rage against was him for hurting me. But now, I want to kill that bitch for ever, ever, hurting you."

Pilot was stunned by her declaration, by the revelation of her terrible past. "If your father wasn't already dead ..."

She smiled grimly. "We both have damage. Together, I know we can make it okay again, beautiful man." Her voice was a whisper now, and although her face showed her youth, her words made her sound more mature than he could ever have expected.

"I adore you," Pilot said. "I adore you, Boheme, and we've known each other what? A week?"

"Time is a human construct. It has nothing to do with love, Pilot Scamo." She tilted her head up to kiss him and his lips crushed against hers.

Boh reached over and switched off the stove, pulling the boiling water from the flame, slipping a lid on the sauce. Pilot watched her, his hands on her waist, and when she looked back at him, he knew what she was doing. "We can have this later, Pilot," she said softly.

"Later?"

She looked up at from beneath her lashes. "After ..."

She took his hand and led him to his bedroom. Her apparent confidence was belied by the fact she was trembling uncontrollably. Pilot nodded. "It's okay," he said, his lips against hers, "I'll show you."

She nodded and lifted her arms for him to slide her sweatshirt over her head. Pilot dropped her top onto the floor, and bent to kiss her mouth, then trailed his lips along her jawbone. His fingers slid under the straps of her bra and drew them down her shoulders. Boh leaned into him as he kissed her shoulders, her collarbone, her throat.

Pilot looked into her face; he could tell she was scared but he could also see the desire in them. "Baby, one word and I'll stop, okay?"

"Don't stop." Her voice was a whisper. Her fingers were in his hair, stroking his dark curls, and he lifted her into his arms, laying her down onto the bed. He slowly unzipped her blue jeans and pulled them off, his hands on her body, stroking her belly. He loved that she wasn't skin and bones, that she had retained her curves even if she was toned and athletic. He pressed his lips against the soft curve of her belly, rimming her navel with his tongue and his hands drew her panties down her legs.

Boh gasped as he moved lower and his mouth found her shaved sex. His tongue lashed around her clit, teasing and probing, and she felt a flood of emotion and pleasure slow through her. He was being gentle, holding back, she knew because he had guessed it was her first consensual time. As his mouth pleasured her, Boh finally let go, tears rolling down her face but with a smile on her face. He made her come, gasping and panting and writhing, and when he moved up the bed to kiss her mouth, she smiled at him through her tears.

Pilot kissed the tears away. "Are you okay?"

"More than, Pilot. More than. These are happy tears, I promise." She reached down and cupped his erection through his jeans. "Please, Pilot ... I want you."

He stripped quickly and rolled a condom down over his impressively big cock. As he hitched her legs around his waist, his eyes were serious. "Remember, you want to stop, we stop."

She pulled his head down to kiss his mouth. "I want you," she repeated and Pilot smiled.

Boh felt a moment of terror as his cock notched into the entrance of her sex but as he slid gently into her, all of her fear left her. God, this man ... As he filled her, his eyes never left hers, searching, questioning. She tightened her thighs around his waist as they began to move, making love slowly at first then as the intensity built between them, harder, faster, deeper.

This time her orgasm shot through her like a bomb, making her cry out, arch her back, beg him to never stop. Bright sparks filled her vision and she gasped for air, wishing this feeling would never end, not caring if she lived or died at that moment.

Pilot groaned as she felt his body spasm with his own climax, and she stroked his face as he recovered, his skin damp with sweat, his smile huge. "God, Boh ..."

Oh, how I love you. But she didn't say it, knowing that kind of declaration was way too soon, even if she knew without a doubt that it was true. "Thank you," she whispered, "you take the pain away."

Pilot chuckled a little incredulously. "Right back at you, gorgeous girl." He kissed her and excused himself to go deal with the used condom. Boh lay on the bed, staring up at the ceiling, trying to process the whirlwind of emotions flooding through her.

When Pilot returned, she held out her arms and he went into them. They kissed, and Boh stroked his face. "You are the most wonderful man."

Pilot laughed softly. "I'm not, but I hope to be for you, Boh."

He lifted her hand and kissed her fingertips. "I have to ask—the age difference doesn't bother you?"

She shook her head. "Like I said, time is a human construct."

"I'm crazy about you, Boheme Dali."

She smiled and kissed him. "Pilot?"

"Yeah, babe?"

Her stomach growled, and they both laughed. "Food now?"

"Food, please."

SHE SWOONED over the perfect little potato pasta dumplings as she scooped the last of her gnocchi into her mouth. "You are a genius."

"Ha, it really is a very simple dish." Pilot leaned over and caught a little glob of marinara sauce next to her mouth with his finger. She grinned at him.

"We keep cleaning each other up."

Pilot laughed. "Strange you should say that because what I've got in mind for us is very, very dirty."

Boh chuckled and slid off of her seat to go to him. He wrapped his arms around her. "Listen, I have news about our project."

He showed her the shots he had sent to Grady Mallory. Boh's eyes were wide. "That's me?"

"That's you, baby. You are luminous in front of the camera." He traced the line of her body on one of the pictures. "Look how much movement you can see just in this shot. You're amazing."

"Yeah, I think it's you who are amazing, Pilot, I—"

Pilot's intercom buzzed, and they looked at each other. Boh felt her heart sink. *Please, please don't let it be that bitch of an ex-wife...*

Sighing, Pilot answered but when he heard the "Hey, loser, let me in," he began to smile.

"It's Romana, my sister," he explained to Boh, "thank God."

Boh hopped off her stool, still alarmed. "Should I go?"

"Hell, no." He waved his hand at her. "Romana will love you. Fair warning, you'll feel like you've been hit by a friendly hurricane."

Boh giggled. "Really? Still," she looked down at her almost naked body, "I might go throw some clothes on."

In the bedroom, she yanked her sweatshirt over her head and pulled on her jeans. She heard voices outside, sounds of greeting, loud Italian being spoken, and shyly went to join the siblings.

Romana Scamo was slender, elegant, but, as Boh was pleased to note, obviously a tomboy too. She and Boh both wore jeans and sweatshirts, but while Boh's hair was long and wavy, Romana had cut her dark hair into a shoulder skimming bob. Her eyes were dark brown, unlike her brother's, but she was as beautiful as her brother. She smiled at Boh as Boh came into the room.

"Hey there, Bella. Pilot's told me all about you." She kissed Boh on each cheek. "It is really good to meet you. Pilot's talked about nothing else but you for a week."

"Ro, don't ruin my game," Pilot said, grinning, and slid his arm around Boh's waist. "Proper introduction. Boheme Dali, prima ballerina, meet Ramona Scamo, irritating sibling and incredible photographer. Almost as good as her brother," he added with a wink and Boh and Romana laughed.

"Don't believe a word of it. I'm better," Ramona shot back, then eyed Boheme critically. "But I would kill to have you in front of my camera."

"Dude, are you hitting on my girlfriend?" Pilot teased his sister, not knowing the effect his words had on Boh.

His girlfriend. Wow.

Her pleasure must have showed as Pilot kissed her temple

and Ramona beamed. "Look, kids, I'm sorry to barge in on your romantic evening, but I was passing by and Pilot promised to show me the photos of you, Boh."

"Which you couldn't have looked at on your email?"

Ramona grinned. "I admit I did, but I was passing by anyway."

"For gossip."

"You caught me."

They all laughed. Boh relaxed. Ramona was as warm and friendly as her brother and as Pilot talked with his sister about the project, Boh felt them including her at every turn, as if she were already part of the family.

"I agree with Grady," Ramona was saying. "No gimmicks. Boh doesn't need them. Look at her ..." She bent to study the photos and then grinned. "You're right. I absolutely am forming quite the crush on you, Boh."

Pilot opened another bottle of wine and they lounged around on his couch, chatting until the early hours. Seeing Boh dropping with exhaustion at nearly two-thirty, Ramona got up and hugged them both goodbye. "Sure I can't drive you home?" Pilot looked concerned but Ramona rolled her eyes.

"Dude, I'm fine. You, lady, come here and hug me. I look forward to getting to know you better."

AFTER SHE LEFT, Boh smiled at Pilot as he led her back to bed. "She's wonderful."

"She's a maniac, but yeah, I do love her. She's very like our mom, a force of nature."

Boh felt a pang at the tenderness with which he spoke about his family and he noticed her reticence. She smiled at him. "It's just ... I wish I'd had that kind of familial love."

"You have it now if you want it."

They didn't make love again, both too exhausted, but they wrapped themselves around the other. "Goodnight, baby."

"Goodnight, my sweet girl."

She nuzzled her nose against his, then his lips were against hers as they fell asleep. As Boh closed her eyes, she wondered if tonight was just the beginning of a new happy life. Could she believe in it? She hoped so.

IN THE MORNING, however, the dizziness came back. Boh and Pilot made love. But he could tell something was off. "Hey, are you okay, baby? We can stop."

Boh shook her head, wanting to be near him despite her whirling mind. "No, please don't."

The nausea kept her from climaxing, however, and she confessed her illness to Pilot. "It's only mild anemia. It just sometimes catches up on me. I'll be okay."

Pilot frowned. "You should take the day, recover."

"Ha," she said, "and find myself out of a job."

"If you're sick, you're sick. They'll understand."

The idea of just lying here and resting or being with Pilot was too tempting, but could she risk Kristof's rage? She sat up and shook her head. Big mistake. Waiting for the dizziness to pass, she leaned into Pilot's arms. "Seriously, I'll be okay in a few minutes. I should go to the studio. It isn't worth Kristof's temper to risk a day off, and he did see us leave together. He'll think I'd rather be in bed with you than dancing with him. Which would be true," she added with a grin.

Pilot still looked worried, but he nodded. "Okay, but I'll drive you in after a huge breakfast, no arguments."

"Sounds good."

After she had showered and dressed, she went into the kitchen and laughed. A plate piled high with steak, spinach, and eggs was waiting for her. "You just happen to have all these iron-rich foods around?" she asked Pilot, who laughed.

"Hey, look, I used to love Popeye. Eat up, Dali."

She ate every bite and regretted it when she saw the food baby in her stomach. "Leotards are unforgiving," she groaned, then grinned. "But that was wonderful, thank you. I probably won't need to eat again for about a week."

"Ha, just try that around me."

She threw her arms around his neck. "Food, sex, art with a beautiful man. I'm the luckiest girl alive."

Pilot smiled, his eyes merry. "Yeah, you are," he drawled, tickling her and making her giggle. "Now, are you sure that you're okay to work today?"

"Positive. I'm Popeye strong now."

"Is that a thing?"

"It is now?"

Pilot chuckled and grabbed his keys. "Come on then, Popeye, let's get you to work."

"You realize that makes you Olive Oyl, right?"

"Does not."

"Does too."

THEY JOKED ALL the way to her work, and Boh was still smiling when she walked into Kristof Mendelev's studio—and into a nightmare.

CHAPTER ELEVEN

"Late again," Kristof barked at her but Boh ignored him. She wasn't late; she had made sure of that. Still her fellow dancers looked beat up already—clearly, Kristof had surprised them.

"You okay?" she mouthed at Elliott, who shook his head. Serena gave her the finger surreptitiously.

"Now, seeing as the rest of you look like a bunch of football players, Boh, I want you to go through the combination for them. Hurry up and change."

Boh had already put her leotard on, so she quickly strapped on her shoes. "Which combination?"

Kristof looked at her. "The combination for the ballet we're doing, Boh." He said the words slowly, as if she was a child, and Boh flushed, annoyed. Bastard.

"We're doing three ballets, Kristof, unless you forgot to count." The words came out of her mouth before she could stop them, and she felt the atmosphere change in the room.

Kristof's eyes took on a dangerous look, but he merely said. "The Lesson. The Pupil's murder. I'll dance the Teacher for the first few times."

Boh knew he wouldn't hold back but she would die before she let him intimidate her. They went through the combinations a few times, Kristof criticizing her at every level. When it came to the murder scene, he would force his fist against her stomach until she felt she would be bruised from the force of it. But she didn't say anything, continuing on and on as he made her rehearse it over and over again.

On the seventh run through, she felt the dizziness return. Push through it, push through it. She danced and kept dancing even as her vision blurred and she felt herself move outside of her body. She heard the rest of them begin to murmur but it sounded like the sound was coming from the end of a very long tunnel. Her ears buzzed, her throat burned. She felt herself falling, then her body was jerking uncontrollably, and she gave in to the darkness as she heard people screaming.

BOH OPENED her eyes to find herself on a hospital gurney being wheeled through the stark white halls of an emergency room. She tried to sit. "Sweetheart, lie down, they're just going to check you out." She heard Nelly Fine's voice and felt comforted. Nelly slipped her hand into Boh's.

Boh opened her mouth, but she found she couldn't speak. What the hell? She knew it had to be the anemia, but she'd never thought it could feel this bad.

While they waited for the doctor, Nelly stroked her hot forehead. "I called Pilot," she said in a low voice, and smiled at Boh. "I know you two are close, and he'd want to know. Grace is also on her way."

Boh felt a pang of loneliness despite her relief that Pilot and Grace were coming. Her boyfriend of a week and her college friend. They represented her family now. When she'd joined the NYSMBC, she'd bonded with Nelly quickly, and over time had asked her to be her next of kin, so Boh had no worries about the hospital contacting her birth family, but still. It was a small group.

Her fears fled though when Pilot and Grace arrived, one after the other, both of them looking fraught, and sighing with relief when they saw her awake. "Thank God." Pilot bent over and kissed her gently. "Are you okay?"

She nodded, but Nelly interjected. "She's having trouble speaking. I think it's just shock at collapsing but I'm no doctor."

Grace, pale and shaken, kissed Boh's cheek. "Hey, baby girl." She and Pilot exchanged a glance. "Nell, I think you should know that Boh was recently diagnosed with mild anemia."

Nell nodded. "I did suspect something was wrong. Did she eat today?"

It was weird that they were talking about her as if she wasn't there, and Boh felt tears spring up in her eyes. She tugged on Pilot's hand and made a motion—she wanted his arms around her. Pilot perched on the edge of the bed, and Boh wriggled into his embrace. Pilot kissed her forehead and looked back at Nell. "She did. We had breakfast this morning."

"Popeye breakfast," Boh managed to croak, and she felt relief that her speech hadn't gone forever. Her fear had been that it was indicative of something more than just the shock of collapsing, and her whole body relaxed.

The doctor came to see them soon after and ran through some tests. He didn't look too concerned. "I would suggest rest, more than anything else. I know how you ballerinas go hard at it, but rest and a good diet will go a long way in your case." He hesitated. "Any other symptoms you're not being forward about?"

"No, I would tell you." Boh was already feeling better.

The doctor nodded and smiled. "I'd like to keep you in overnight just to make sure, but I'm leaving that up to you."

"Honestly, I'd feel better at home." She tried to smile. "I don't do well in hospitals."

He patted her leg. "Fine. I assume there'll be someone with you?"

"Yes," Pilot and Grace both answered at the same time and broke into laughter.

The doctor grinned. "Well, I'll leave you two to fight over this one." He smiled at Boh kindly. "Take care of yourself, Boh. My wife and I are great fans of the ballet."

"You'll have the best seats at our next show," Nelly told him, and he laughed.

"I should say no," he lowered his voice to a stage-whisper, "but I won't. Goodnight, folks."

Pilot sat down next to Boh again. "So, where's home for you tonight? No pressure either way."

Grace grinned. "Dudes, why not both of you stay at our place? Show Mr. Showbiz here the way real people live. I'm going back to the studio to practice my piece for the performance on Friday, so you'll have privacy."

Pilot laughed and Boh was pleased to see her two friends bonding. "Well, if you don't mind squeezing into a single bed?" She looked at Pilot, who grinned.

"With you? I'd sleep under a bridge. Sleep, baby," he added meaningfully and Boh flushed, unable to stop the grin on her face.

He took her home, and as they climbed the stairs to the apartment, she noticed a box of groceries outside the door, as well as several bouquets of flowers. Pilot smiled as he hefted the boxes and flowers inside. "The food is from me—well, the doc did say you needed to eat—and the flowers are from your friends. Even Kristof," he said with a sigh as he checked the card on a huge bunch of lilies. "Lovely. Send funeral flowers, asshole."

"No matter," she said, and dumped the lilies in the trash. "We can't have lilies in the house because of Beelzebub."

Pilot stopped. "Beelzebub?" His tone was incredulous and Boh giggled. She really was feeling better now, and she went to find the malevolent cat. She picked him up and took him out to meet Pilot.

"Pilot Scamo, meet Beelzebub. He earns his name." The cat was already yowling to get out of her grip, but as she dumped him on Pilot, the cat suddenly calmed and rubbed Pilot's chin with his head.

"You damn little turncoat," she laughed as Pilot looked smug. He stroked the cat then put him gently down and looked around the apartment.

"This place is great."

Boh chuckled. "You don't have to say that."

"No, I mean it. First up, bookshelves stuffed with books. Always the mark of good character." He grinned as he spoke. "Do you know that John Waters quote?"

"If you go home with someone and they don't have books, don't fuck them," she answered and he laughed. Boh slid her arms round his waist. "It's a good rule of thumb."

Pilot kissed her. "Are you hungry?"

"Not really, but I should eat something." She looked over at the box of groceries. "What did you buy me?"

Pilot grinned. "Well, for tonight, I thought maybe scrambled eggs with a little truffle oil?"

Boh moaned. "God, truffle oil, you seductive little tramp."

Pilot made them both plates of eggs and when Boh put the first bite in her mouth, she almost swooned. "Geez, Scamo, is there nothing you can't do?"

"You asked that before and believe me, the answer's the

same," but he smiled and took her hand. "Sweetheart, you will rest over the next couple of days, right? Nelly's clearing it with the ballet company, but I'm not telling you what to do. I'm just concerned."

"This was nothing, really, but I take your point. Don't tell anyone but I'm actually kind of relieved to get some time." She smiled shyly. "If you're around, maybe we can work on some ideas for the exhibition."

"I'm not going anywhere." He stroked his hand over her face. "You look exhausted."

"I'm okay." But a half-hour later, the day's events caught up with her and they lay down on her tiny single bed, Boh cradled in his arms. She was asleep before they'd even finished saying goodnight.

P‍ILOT LAY AWAKE LONG after Boh's breathing became steady and he knew she was out. He had been so worried but at the same time, he was angry at Kristof. If the man was working Boh too hard as revenge on her for being with Pilot ...

Don't be paranoid. Kristof and Eugenie had been the ones cheating, not him, so if anyone had the right to be vengeful it was Pilot ... but that wasn't him.

Unless Kristof hurt Boh. Pilot had to be honest—he hated the idea of this ballet Kristof was putting together. It sounded cruel and sadistic, but what did he know?

He looked down at Boh in his arms. She looked so young and not for the first time, he wondered if he was doing the right thing by dating her. There was almost 20 years between them. He was grateful for Ramona, Nell, and Grace's support— but that didn't mean he was good for Boh.

The thought of not being with her was painful though and so, for now, he told himself, he would be selfish. They could work things out as they came along—wasn't that how relationship worked? Relationships of equals?

Despite his age, his experience, after being married to Eugenie, Pilot still felt he was new at this. He wouldn't tell Boh that, however, because he wanted her to feel as if he was her rock, and he would be. He just had to learn how to do this too.

He heard his phone buzz from the other room. He gently extracted himself, trying not to wake Boh. He sighed when he saw it was Eugenie calling. "Christ."

He debated turning his phone off, but maybe he could head her off at the pass. "Hey, Genie."

She was crying and Pilot could tell instantly that she was drunk. "Pilot ... can you come? I just feel so low. I don't know what I'll do."

"What's happened?"

She hesitated and he knew she was just trying to make excuses. "I'm lonely, Pilot. Ever since you left me ... God, I just feel wretched."

Pilot listened to her and found himself unmoved. "Genie, call your mom. Call your sister. This is not my problem anymore."

"Be sweet, baby." God, had her voice always been this grating? He said nothing, letting her rant.

"We could try again," she said, "there'll always be a history between us now, always a connection. I think about you all of the time, and I really think, if we tried again, we could be happy. I miss you, baby, your gorgeous face, your eyes, your big cock. I dream about you fucking me so hard, like the way we did when we first got together."

Jesus. "Genie, it's late and I have to work tomorrow."

There was a silence. "Are you with another woman?"

God help him, he wanted to hurt her. "I'm with my girlfriend. I have to go."

Eugenie reacted exactly how he thought she would, an explosion of vitriol that he had heard before. He ended the call with her in mid-rant. Yeah, he was definitely going to look for a new apartment. He called his sister. Ramona was a night owl, like him.

"Hey, dude."

He told her what had happened with Boh, reassuring her that she was okay, then told her about Genie's call. Ramona sighed. "That bitch ... is she ever going to get the message? Seriously, bro, you need to ghost her entirely. Change your phone, your address, everything."

"I agree. Everything apart from the studio—she never knew about that to begin with."

"Sure? She's obviously keeping tabs on you, and it's not like she doesn't have the money to hire private dicks to tail you."

"I'm sure."

"You all set for the exhibit? I talked to Grady. He's really excited, based on the photos of Boh you sent. Listen, he asked me to, um, maybe do the next benefit for the Foundation ... but I told him I wouldn't commit without speaking to you first."

Pilot was astonished. "Why? Ro, this is a huge opportunity; you need to call him back right now ..." he checked his watch, "It's only nine p.m. in Seattle."

Ramona laughed. "Dude, chill. I'll call him in the morning." She chuckled, then Pilot heard her hesitating. "Is Boh really okay? I hear horror stories of how those dancers are treated."

"She's tougher than you think. A little anemia and an asshole like Mendelev are nothing to what she's overcome in her life. Ro?"

"Yeah?"

"You think I'm too old for her?"

"Shut up."

He snorted with laughter. "Say what you mean, sis."

"I'm selfish. I haven't seen you happier with someone ... ever. Even if it's only been what, a week?"

"Is everything too fast?"

"Dude, come on. What's fast? You met, you were attracted, you went to the next level. It's not like you're moving in together."

After Ramona had said goodbye, Pilot felt his body relax. He turned off his phone and went back to bed. Boh stirred as he curved himself around her. "Pilot?"

"I'm here, baby," he said, "I'm here."

KRISTOF WAS, as always, in a foul mood and there was the fact that he was here, in this toilet cubicle, lifting the lid to the cistern and not finding the small vial of urine he was expecting. He heard someone come into the bathroom and trying to get into his stall. Kristof opened the door and pulled Elliott into the stall. "You're late, fuck nut."

Elliott didn't seem remotely bothered. He handed Kristof the sample. "Were you worried, Kristof?"

"Don't talk back, you little asshole."

Elliott's eyes narrowed. "Your supply could always dry up, Kristof. Remember that next time you torture Boh into a hospital bed."

Kristof laughed humorlessly. "So that's what this little tantrum is about? Your girlfriend?"

"My friend, and yes. You do that to her again and I'll go straight to Liz."

"You're threatening me, you little punk? You'll never dance again if you tell anyone about our little arrangement."

Elliott squared his shoulders. He was shorter than Kristof by almost a foot, but he stood his ground. "To stop your bullying, I'd do it. Remember that, asshole."

He stalked out of the stall, Kristof on his heel, ready to argue again. They both stopped when they saw Eleonor Vasquez looking at them quizzically. Her eyes lit on the urine sample in Kristof's hand and he went cold.

Eleonor's eyes fluttered around the room. "This isn't my studio."

Elliott took her arm. "No, Madam Vasquez. Would you like me to take you to it?"

She smiled at him. "Nureyev. Are you him?"

"I wish, Madam Vasquez," Elliott grinned. "It's Elliott, remember?"

Eleonor didn't answer. She was looking at Kristof. "I know you."

Kristof, the urine sample now firmly behind his back, nodded. "Eleonor." Thank God she had dementia, he thought. Maybe she wouldn't have known what was happening between him and Elliott. If Celine, or Nell had walked in ...

He watched Elliott lead Vasquez out of the bathroom and felt the energy sap from his body. A close call. Maybe he should tone it down for a few days. When Boh came back, he'd go easy on her. He knew she knew the ballets like the back of her hand and if push came to shove, she could be off for a week and still be ready.

It pissed him off that she was with Scamo. His Boh was with that man ... Kristof took credit for Boh's talent entirely and to have her so far out of his control ... no. Keep calm. She'll come back.

For now, his bigger problem was if Eleonor had a lucid moment and was able to process what she had seen. It wouldn't take a genius to figure out what he was doing and if she told Celine, it would be the end of him personally and professionally. Kristof found his hands were shaking and screwed them into fists. There was a way to deal with this, but he didn't know if he had the guts to follow through. If he silenced Eleonor, he could never go back. For now, he knew, he was just a junkie asshole with an ego the size of a planet. Immoral but not … he swallowed hard. No, I am not even considering this.

He swiped the urine sample, poured it into his own marked container, and replaced the original back in the cistern. He would come off the drugs, clear out his system. Hopefully, if and when Eleonor remembered, he would be submitting his own urine for drug testing and none of this would make any difference. He would be kinder to Elliott too, the little weasel. Satisfied he had this under control, he left the bathroom and went to begin his day.

SERENA SLITHERED around the corner with a smile on her face. So, it was Elliott's pee Kristof was using to pass his drug testing. She had been passing the bathroom and heard the argument inside. Good. Now she had that in her back pocket too.

Serena only had one thing she wanted to achieve and that was being principal. She had almost been there and then Boheme Dali came along. Well, if she couldn't get there by talent, she'd use other means.

Blackmail being one of them.

She grinned to herself and went to her next class.

12

CHAPTER TWELVE

It had been two days since her collapse, and Boh was rested and relieved it hadn't taken her longer to recover. She had spent the last two days with Pilot, and now, they were back in his studio, working on the exhibition photographs.

Boh had asked the ballet company's clothes director if she could borrow some costumes, and Arden had come through for her with some incredible outfits, some traditional, like the costume for the white swan, some not so traditional.

For now, though, she wore a simple light pink leotard, her hair down and slightly damp, and she posed around the studio. Right now, she was en pointe on top of an old shipping crate as Pilot moved around her, clicking away. The studio lights were hot but Boh didn't care.

"Okay, baby, you can get down now." Pilot grinned at her, then stared down at his camera, flicking through the images. She loved to watch him work. It was as if the sadness she saw constantly in his eyes evaporated and he became this other being, Pilot, the photographer.

Her love.

She padded over to him and slid an arm around his waist as

he showed her what they had created. She chuckled softly. "I'll never get over the fact that that's me. You are a genius."

She looked up to find him gazing at her and a thrill went through her body. His eyes were soft with love, full of desire. "Hey, pretty girl," he said softly and brushed his lips against hers. God, he was intoxicating. Pilot put his camera down and took her in his arms. "How are you feeling?"

Boh smiled. "So, so much better, Pilot ... so much better."

His lips crushed against hers and she tangled her fingers in his dark curls as they kissed, the heat between them a firestorm. Pilot peeled her leotard from her shoulders, pulling it down so he could take her nipples into his mouth in turn. The feel of his tongue on her nipple made her moan with pleasure and she took his hand and pressed it between her legs. "I'm so wet for you, baby ..."

With a groan, Pilot swept her onto the floor and covered her body with his. He tugged her leotard off and kicked out of his jeans as Boh pulled his T-shirt over his head. She couldn't get enough of this man's body, the way he made her feel so precious, so beautiful. She ran her hands over his hard chest and looked up into his eyes. The way he looked at her ...

"You're so beautiful," she whispered and he chuckled.

"Stealing my best lines ..." His lips were against her again then as she wrapped her legs around his waist, and they began to make love slowly, taking their time.

The feel of his cock inside her, filling her, made her moan with uninhibited pleasure. Boh kissed his soft lips with such passion, she tasted blood. Pilot braced his arms on either side of her head and thrust harder as they both neared climax, Boh encouraging him harder, deeper.

She came, arching her back, pressing her belly against his as she felt his body judder and jerk with his own climax. They collapsed next to each other, panting, and Boh giggled.

"We're animals."

Pilot laughed, his face flushed pink from his exertions. "That we are. God, Boh, you make me feel like a new man. Shit, that was so cliché, but it's true. I've never felt like this before. Ever."

Her body tingled with delight at his words. "Really?"

"Really." He turned onto his side and trailed a fingertip down her body, making her wriggle with pleasure. He stroked her belly, then bent his head to press his lips against the smooth curve of it. He looked up at her, questioning, and she nodded as he smiled and moved down her body.

He pushed her thighs apart and then his mouth was on her sex, licking, teasing, sucking. His fingers massaged the skin of her inner thighs as she felt the excitement build again from the depths of her body, making her skin tingle, her limbs liquify.

Pilot made her come again and again, then, shyly, she told him she wanted to return the favor. "You have to tell me if I'm doing this wrong."

She took his cock into her mouth, flicking her tongue over the sensitive tip. She was gratified when Pilot sucked in a shaky breath and told her. "That's it, like that, baby." She trailed her tongue up and down the silky shaft, her hands massaging his sack. His cock, huge, thick, and long, quivered at her touch, stiffening until Pilot was gasping and groaning.

"Baby, I'm close if you want to stop?"

Boh shook her head, instead wanting to swallow his seed down. Pilot came and she felt his semen pump into her tongue, a sweet yet salty taste.

Afterwards, they showered together, and ordered pizza. While they waited, they sat on the couch and went through his photos. Pilot chuckled to himself. "You know what? I think we almost have an exhibit, baby. I've never known someone to be as affecting as you on camera. I would like some outside shots too, plus some of you working at the barre in class."

"Shouldn't be a problem." She nudged him with her shoulder. "Listen, Grace is in Rubies tonight at the Lincoln Center. I'd like to go and support her ... wanna come?"

"Hell, yes. You know, I have a confession."

Boh grinned at the mischievous look in his eyes. "Oh, yes?"

"When I was married to Genie, we used to go to the ballet ... but as soon as they started, I would go off and do something else. I've never actually seen a performance."

"Pilot Tiffany Scamo, you dirty rotten scoundrel!"

Pilot busted out laughing. "Tiffany?"

"What, it's Richard Gere's middle name." Boh shrieked with laughter as Pilot tickled her into submission. "Anyway, what is your middle name?"

"Joseph. Yours?"

"I don't have one." Boh nibbled at his earlobe as he pulled her onto his lap. "So, you've never seen a ballet, huh?"

"Nope. But to answer your original question, yes, I'd love to come to Rubies with you. I'll get us a box."

"Fancy." She kissed his cheek as he snagged the phone from his pocket and called the Lincoln Center, grinning as he dropped his name without hesitation.

"One box reserved for Mr. Pilot Scamo and his beautiful guest, superstar ballerina, Boheme Dali."

Boh stroked his curls away from his face, his devastatingly handsome face, and kissed him gently. "His lover, Boh, thanks Mr. Pilot Scamo, and asks politely if he wouldn't mind very much fucking her again, right here, right now."

Pilot grinned as he laid her back on the couch. "Anything the prima wants, the prima gets ..." and they began to make love again.

Kristof poured himself a mug of coffee and looked up as

Celine Peletier entered the staffroom. She nodded to him, unsmiling as always. Miserable bitch. He'd never liked the other woman, probably because Celine was the most exquisite dancer he'd ever seen, and she knew her shit now as a teacher. Plus, the company of dancers adored her, even when she was at her most strident.

Also, he knew Celine thought of him as a boy, an amateur despite his prestigious career. His heroes—Baryshnikov, Nureyev, Vasiliev—all had careers after dancing and Kristof wanted his to be as impressive as theirs. He knew Celine, Nell, Liz … none of them believed he was at that standard, but he was determined to prove them wrong.

"Good morning, Celine."

She looked up as if she was deep in thought. "Kristof. Oh, I hear I'm to thank you."

"Because?"

"Elliott told me you and he managed to reroute Eleonor back to her studio a few afternoons ago. I do hope she wasn't intruding on … anything."

Kristof went cold. She knew. "No, not at all," he said, keeping his expression blank.

"Well, thank you." She sighed and sat down opposite him. "Eleonor is getting more and more confused. I think it may be time for her for give up her teaching all together."

"That's a tragedy," Kristof said carefully. His body relaxed a little. "After such an illustrious career."

"Indeed." Celine stared out of the window and Kristof was astonished to see tears in her eyes. "They call it sundowning; did you know that? Such a pretty name for such a terrible thing. Eleonor has her moments of clarity but they are less and less. Sometimes she will remember the most random things from weeks and weeks ago and she'll talk with absolute surety about them. Then the next moment ..." Celine made a motion in the air. "Nothing. Sorry, Kristof, it's none of your concern."

The constricting fear had already returned and he just nodded stiffly as Celine left the room, but he didn't have a moment to process what he'd learned because Liz's secretary came to find him. "She wants to see you."

TEN MINUTES later he walked out of Liz's office, stunned. Not only had she told him that his Sex and Death showcase was being moved from their own theater to the Metropolitan Opera, but that she had authorized a bigger budget for ... everything. Sets, costumes ... he had free rein.

Kristof had shaken his head in disbelief. "Why?"

"We've had a significant donation—anonymous. But on the condition that you are given a large part of it for your new piece. You have a fan, Kristof."

He should have felt elated; after all, wasn't this every choreographer's dream? But now, knowing what he knew about Eleonor Vasquez ... she could bring it all down. All of it.

He couldn't let that happen. He knew what he had to do.

CHAPTER THIRTEEN

Pilot look appreciatively at Boh in her gown and whistled. "Damn, woman ... how am I supposed to concentrate when you look like that?"

Boh smiled shyly. Her dress was simple in design, but the midnight-blue fabric and heavy beading around the bodice sparkled like stars at midnight, throwing little beams of light up into her face. "It's just off the rack. It's my go-to for events. Old thing, really."

Pilot's expression was lustful. "Boh ... you're so beautiful it hurts."

She giggled. "Right back at you, handsome." He was wearing a black tux with a bowtie, his beard neatly clipped back but his curls still messy. Boh kissed him. "The car's here."

In the car, he asked her about the ballet. "So, what's the story of the ballet?"

"Well, to start with, there's no story as such. The full ballet is in three parts—it's called Jewels. But Rubies is the one we all love to dance. It's very modern, abstract ... I can see I'm losing you already," Boh joked, seeing his confused face. "Just concentrate on admiring the movement, the shapes they make with their bodies. I think, as a photographer, you'll find it fascinating."

Pilot nodded, trying to look convinced, but Boh could see he was a little bemused. She kissed him. "Just go with it. We're here to support Grace anyway."

In the foyer, Boh recognized some of her colleagues from the company, and she introduced them to Pilot again, most of them looking at him with curious, admiring eyes. Boh was grateful at the ease with which he chatted to them.

Elliott found her and grinned. "That man is crazy about you," he said. "He hasn't stopped talking about you since you got here."

Boh flushed pink, a thrill going through her. "He is the most wonderful man," she said in a low voice, then stopped. She saw Kristof and Serena across the bar, talking in low tones. Boh sighed. "I see Cruella and his lapdog are here."

Elliott looked around and his expression hardened. "Have you heard? Kristof's been given carte blanche over the showcase. They've moved to the Metropolitan."

"No way." Boh was stunned. "Really?"

"Liz thinks a bigger venue will bring in the cash injection we need."

"But I thought you said ..."

"That donation was specifically for Kristof. Wonder how many city types he had to blow for that?"

Boh didn't know whether to laugh or gag, but she had to admit; the move to the Metropolitan would be good for her career too.

As the ballet began, she and Pilot made their way to their box and settled in. Boh looked around the theater, gratified to see it sold out for her friend's performance. "Rubies is the second part," she whispered to Pilot, who put his arm around her shoulders and pulled her close.

"Do I have to concentrate for the other two parts or can we make out in those sections?" He had a wide grin on his face and she giggled.

"Depends how you behave," she quipped back then sighed, snuggling into his arms. "My two favorite things in the world, you and ballet. Goodnight."

Pilot laughed. "How long is this thing anyway?"

Boh rolled her eyes. "So impatient. Wait and see."

Soon the lights went down and the performance began.

EUGENIE RADCLIFFE-MORGAN STARED UNSEEING at the stage. The ballet had been the one time that her demons calmed and she lost herself in the pure art of it ... but now that Pilot had found himself a new model, a ballerina, Eugenie felt betrayed.

When she'd seen them together, downstairs, in the foyer, she'd almost screamed. Instead she'd excused herself politely from her date and had gone to the restrooms. A bump of cocaine and she'd felt an icy calm descend.

Now, she watched them, wrapped in each other in the box across from hers, and the anger was consuming. Her Pilot with a dancer whore ... and goddamn if he didn't look happy. More than happy, he looked besotted, excited ... in love.

Her date muttered something into her ear and she gave a distracted smile. He—what was his name again? Seth? Saul? — he had approached her at a brunch for a children's charity last week and they had talked. She liked that he looked a little like Pilot and had taken him back to her apartment and fucked him. She'd even enjoyed it, especially when she closed her eyes and pretended he was Pilot.

God, how the hell had she ever let him go? She watched him

now, laughing and kissing that damn girl—he looked ten years younger.

She looked away, sickened. Her eyes swept the other box. Ah, she saw Kristof Mendelev also watching his star dancer and her ex-husband. Kristof sensed her gaze and nodded at her. She saw the same jealousy that she felt reflected in his face. Interesting. He might be a useful ally.

On the other hand ... it had been her fling with Kristof which had finally given Pilot the courage to leave her. It had been the final straw, and as far as Eugenie was concerned, not worth it. It had taken the coked-up Kristof an age to get it up enough to fuck her, and even then, it had been a quick, disappointing coupling. He was handsome, yes, but nothing compared to Pilot. She had been trying to make Pilot jealous and not only had she failed, but she had lost him.

She wasn't stupid enough to think he would ever come back to her, but that didn't mean she intended to let him go. Or end up happy and in love with another woman.

No. Pilot Scamo would not get his happy ever after. They were just for fairy tales.

As GRACE TOOK to the stage, Boh leaned forward and Pilot watched her face change to one of wonder. He loved that she adored her friend's dancing so much, that there wasn't a spitefully competitive bone in her body. He turned his attention towards the stage now. If he was honest, he had no idea what constituted a good ballet, but Boh was right when she told him to concentrate on what the dancers were doing with their bodies. Some of it was quite astonishing, and he found himself thinking of ways he could capture that movement, that flow in his camera. He still had to complete his commitment to the ballet for their publicity shots, and this ballet was helping him how to understand their bodies better.

He stroked Boh's back and she smiled at him. "Enjoying yourself?"

"Always, with you."

She leaned into him, her eyes on the stage. "Look at her, Pilot. She's sensational."

They watched Grace during the short ballet and when she took her bow, they both stood and applauded her. She saw them in the box and gave them a wave and a grin as she left the stage.

"Whoop, whoop," Boh said happily as they retook their seats for the final part, Diamonds. Pilot loved that she was so excited. His eyes drifted around the room, and his heart sank. Eugenie was staring at them. Seeing his scrutiny, she gave him a sarcastic wave. Pilot looked away, annoyed. Goddamn that woman; couldn't he have one night without a reminder of her?

"Boh?"

She looked around at him. "Yeah, babe?"

"How would you feel about moving in with me?"

She blinked, obviously taken aback. "What?"

"I'm looking for a new apartment, somewhere ... new. A new life, with you. If it's too soon, say so, and honestly, that's fair enough. But I'd like you to consider it, if you would."

Boh's eyes were a little troubled. "I will think about it, Pilot. I promise."

But he could tell she was a little discombobulated by his request and he couldn't quite believe he'd made it himself. What was he thinking? They'd been dating for less than a month.

But something in his gut told him it was right, that this was it for him. Careful now, there was a time when you thought the same thing about Genie. He gave a snort. No. He'd never felt that way about his ex-wife. Ever. Looking back now, Genie had done all the running, eventually wearing him down until he dated her, then proposing to him. He'd balked, then she'd played the oldest trick in the book—the unplanned, fictitious pregnancy. He'd been distraught when she'd "lost" it. Only after the divorce had been finalized had she told him there never was any baby. By then, all he'd felt was relief; one thing less to tie him to her.

AFTER THE BALLET ENDED, they had a drink with Grace and her fellow dancers, then Pilot took Boh back to his apartment. "About earlier," he said as they walked into it, "I didn't mean to freak you out. It's just ... put it this way. I'm looking for a new apartment, somewhere my ex-wife knows nothing about. I'd like it if you were to come with me, give me your opinion on the places, help me choose somewhere that, maybe, one day you could see yourself living too. Whether that's this weekend or five years in the future ..."

Boh rolled her eyes, grinning. "Dude, chill, I'll move in with you."

For a second, he didn't process what she'd said, and now Boh began to laugh at his confusion. "You will?"

"Yes, you doofus!" He picked her up and swung her around, utterly joyful.

"Put me down, you big lug," she laughed and when he had set her on her feet, she took his face in her hands. "I love you, Pilot Scamo. I am so in love with you. Of course, I'll move in with you, regardless of how stupid-fast this is."

Pilot could hardly speak. "You love me?"

"Utterly, completely, truly, madly, deeply, all the adverbs, all of 'em, and—" She didn't get to finish her sentence before his lips were against hers, his arms around her tightly.

He lifted her into his arms and carried her into the bedroom. Not wanting to ruin her ballgown, he unzipped the back slowly and she stepped out of the layers of tulle. She pulled at his bowtie, pretended to blindfold him with it, then threw it to one side. "I have to see your eyes," she said, "they're so beautiful. When you look at me like that ... God, Pilot ..."

She pulled his shirt from his pants and he grinned. "Impatient girl."

"I want you naked ..." She looked up at him from underneath long, thick lashes. "I want to go on top tonight, Pilot Scamo."

They stripped each other quickly, and Boh straddled him, stroking his cock against her belly, rolling the condom down it, caressing his balls, then running hands over his stomach. Pilot felt his muscles contracting under her touch. In the faint moonlight, her body looked like gold, her full breasts gently bouncing as she moved. He ran a fingertip between her breasts, down her stomach until it dipped into her navel. She shivered with pleasure at his touch.

"I love you," he said simply. "I think I might have loved you from the first time we talked. I've never had this connection with anyone. You're amazing."

"I'm just me," she said softly, but he could see tears in her eyes. "But I love you too, big boy."

Trust her to make him laugh. "Goofy."

"Doofus." She knelt and guided his cock inside her, moaning as he filled her sweet, velvety cunt. "God, Pilot, I'll never get tired of this, of making love with you." She rode him gently at first, then as his hand snaked between her legs to stroke her clit, she quickened her pace, driving her hips hard against his. He gripped her buttocks hard and she moved faster as her excitement built.

"Christ, you're so beautiful," he panted as she impaled herself hard on his cock and laced her fingers with his. He watched her come, a delicious blush in her cheeks, her skin dewy with sweat, her back arching, her head thrown back. She is a goddess...

Pilot went to sleep that night knowing his future was in his arms.

SERENA WAITED until Kristof was well and truly loaded before calling a cab and loading him and herself into it. She gave the driver directions back to Kristof's apartment and kissed Kristof all the way to stop him objecting.

Once inside, she managed to get him into the apartment and strip him but try as she might, she could not get him hard.

"Stop," Kristof moaned, turning his face into his pillow.

Serena sighed and got off him. "I need a bump."

"Help yourself," Kristof mumbled, groaning. "I feel like shit."

Serena hoovered a line of cocaine up her nostril. "I'll make you some coffee. We need to talk."

"Coffee, then talk. Maybe."

Serena went into Kristof's vast kitchen to crank up his espresso machine. She stood at the floor-to-ceiling window and looked out over Manhattan. Serena placed her hands against the glass. Oh, to be able to afford a place like this. Maybe if she were useful to Kristof, he'd move her in with him permanently.

Maybe if she gave him whatever he wanted. She smirked to herself. They were about to have a very significant chat.

She made the coffee and took it back into the bedroom. Kristof had sat up now, and he actually thanked her for the drink. "What do you want to talk about?"

Serena very deliberately sipped her coffee before answering. "How about the fact that Vasquez caught you and Elliott ... swapping fluids, as it were?"

Kristof went very still, his eyes hooded and dangerous. "What the hell are you talking about?"

"Come on, Kris, I know you've been swapping out your sample for Elliott's. Homeboy is so pure and virginial, he's probably never even heard of cocaine. That's why you picked him and I say ... kudos. The regime at the ballet company can go suck it. You're a genius."

Kristof was silent for a few minutes, studying Serena. Eventually, he lifted his chin. "What is it you want, Serena? If you're looking for principal ... I'm sorry. In all conscience, you're not ready for that."

"Fine."

He looked at her quizzically. "Fine? Now I am intrigued. What could you possibly want more than principal?"

Serena smiled. "You. I want you. Us. Together. Personally and professionally. I want to be your lover and your muse. I want to be your partner."

Kristof snorted but then his eyes got serious. "Serena, because I like you, I'll be honest. Look at me. I'm an almost 50-year-old junkie has-been. Why the fuck would you want me? I'm not even that rich. You're young, beautiful, and you could find yourself a sugar daddy like that." He clicked his fingers.

"But I don't want a sugar daddy, Kris." She went to sit by his side. "I don't want money, although this place is sweet." Serena slipped her hand into his and was gratified that he didn't pull away. "Why should she get the mentor, the billionaire photographer, the lead, the spotlight in everything? You know I'm as good as she is."

"So, that's what this is about—Boh."

Serena pressed her lips to his fiercely. "She's not the only girl in the world."

Kristof put down his coffee cup and pulled her onto his lap. Serena wriggled, feeling his cock respond at last. Kristof ran his hands through her hair. "You're not as good as Boh is and you know that. But you could be."

"With the right mentor."

He moved suddenly, flipping her onto her back and kicking her legs apart. He thrust his cock deep inside her, trying to regain some of the power which seemed to have shifted. "And what would you be prepared to do for that?"

Serena smiled up at him. "Anything, Kristof ... I would do anything."

CHAPTER FOURTEEN

Boh tried not to look too enamored with the loft space they were looking at, but she saw the same excitement in Pilot's eyes. The loft, three blocks from the ballet company, was vast, open plan, exposed red brick, and huge windows. Boh's eyes were wide with the possibilities. Was this really her life now?

The realtor left them alone to talk and Pilot wrapped his arms around her. "Can you see it, Boh? The bookshelves along that wall, our bed over there ..."

"It's perfect," she said, and turned in his arms to kiss him. "It's perfect, except ... there's no way I'll even be able to half match you in price."

Pilot looked surprised. "That's not something you need to worry about."

"But it is. For one thing, it's not fair on you. For another, I do not want to be a kept woman."

"A kept woman? Boh, all we're talking about is buying a place for us to live. What's mine is yours. Are you really going to put what other people might think above our happiness?"

Boh shook her head. "No. But I'm paying you rent."

"Fine, if that's what'll do it." Pilot looked around. "But I feel it. This is the place."

Boh laughed softly. "We're going a lot on gut instinct, aren't we?"

"It's a good thing."

Pilot talked to the realtor. "We'll take it, and if the buyer will settle by the end of the week, there'll be a significant bonus."

"I'm sure we can arrange something."

Piot and Boh walked down to one of their favorite burger joints for lunch, hand in hand. As they tucked into their food, Pilot studied Boh. "You're preoccupied."

She smiled at him. "I am, but I'm not having second thoughts, I swear. Taking stock, everything seems to be happening at once. You and me, the showcase, the exhibition."

"Just take one thing at a time. We're good, you and me. The exhibition just needs one or two more shots, a few more candids, I think. Like that image of you right now with burger juice running down your chin." He grinned as she hurriedly mopped her face with a napkin.

Boh chuckled. "The more I think about the exhibition, the more nervous I get. I mean, are they really going to be blown away just by my photos, however brilliantly they are taken?"

"You don't get it, do you? The life, the beauty you bring to my work, it's transcendent. Full disclosure: I fully intend to make you the focus of my work for the next few years." He grinned wickedly and, flushing, she laughed.

"Machiavelli."

"You know it. Speaking of Machiavelli ... how's it going with Mendelev?"

It had been two weeks since she'd collapsed in Kristof's

class, and since then he had been—not kind, exactly—but he hadn't pushed her too hard. Boh knew the steps automatically now, and so Kristof had focused on her and Elliott's chemistry and fluidity. He'd even told them he was happy with The Lesson segment, and moved on to La Sylphide, as well as prepping Serena and Jeremy for Romeo and Juliet.

Boh had been getting home at a decent hour now, but she told Pilot now, she didn't trust this calmer Kristof. "It's just not him. Even when we have no showcase coming up, he's a monster, driving us until we're exhausted. He's up to something."

Plot nodded, knowing the feeling well. Eugenie hadn't called him for a couple of weeks now, and he couldn't help but feel paranoid about it. He told himself that maybe she'd finally got the message that he wasn't coming back to her—but he knew Genie too well.

He sighed, rubbing his head, wishing life was easier, that they could be left alone to enjoy their new love. Boh asked him what he was thinking about and he told her.

She nodded. "I know, baby, but that's not the way the world works."

He smiled at her. "As long as I have you, I'm good."

"Always." Boh cupped his cheek in her hand. "But I hate what she's done to you, Pilot. I can see the damage. A man like you, a strong, courageous, wonderful man like you—it's not fair. I wish I could wave a magic wand and make her leave you alone for good."

Pilot turned his head and kissed her palm. "Don't worry about it. One day, it'll come to me, the way to make her finally get the message that it's over."

"I love you," Boh said, "and it makes me want to protect you."

"I feel the same way, darling, I do. It gives me strength to know you're on my side."

They kissed, not caring what the other patrons of the restaurant thought of their PDA. Afterwards, Pilot walked Boh back to the studio. "Enjoy your class, baby. Shall I come pick you up?"

"Where will you be this afternoon? The Studio?"

"Yep."

Boh kissed him. "Then I'll walk to you. Don't interrupt your work."

They said goodbye and she watched him walk away. He kept turning to smile at her.

"How very romantic," came a droll voice from behind Boh.

Boh turned and gave Serena the finger.

"Keep your jealousy in check, bitch," she muttered as she went inside the building. She sighed when she realized Serena was following her. "What do you want?"

"Oh, nothing, just on my way to grab my stuff from the changing room. And to tell you Kristof is out this afternoon, sick. Celine is taking the rehearsal."

"See, you can give good news as well as bad." Boh wondered why Serena was being so forthcoming. "What's wrong with Kristof?"

"Where do you want me to start?"

Despite her dislike of Serena, Boh actually sniggered at that. She studied the redhead. "I thought you and he …"

"Oh, we are. Doesn't mean I'm blind to his faults. I'd have to be dumb, and if I'm a lot of things, I'm not dumb."

"No, you're not," Boh said and Serena looked surprised.

"Please tell me we're not bonding, Dali." But she had a smile on her face.

Boh snorted. "We're not. But that doesn't mean we can't try to get along. Showcase is coming up; we all need each other."

Serena made a noncommittal sound. She grabbed her bag from the changing room as Boh began to change. "Later, Dali."

"Later."

. . .

ALONE, Boh wondered at Serena. When she had first joined the company, three months after Boh, Serena had appeared to be shy and retiring. Her inner bitch hadn't come out until she'd realized that Boh was on the fast track to principal; Boh had gotten the impression that Serena was used to getting everything she wanted, when she wanted, and to be fair to the other dancer, Serena was a talented dancer. More than talented, she was a natural, but something was missing. Warmth. Connection, both to her partner and her audience. It was the difference between soloist and principal.

Boh smiled at Celine as she entered the studio. "Good afternoon, Madam Peletier."

Celine's eyes softened. "Boh, ma chère, welcome. We're just running through La Sylphide. Warm up and then we'll go through the combinations."

As always, as she began to dance, Boh lost herself in the movement, the technicality, and the beauty of the dance. La Sylphide was one of her favorite ballets to dance and with Vlad, the ethereal Russian, as her partner, Boh soon found herself deeply into the character.

An hour later, however, a very pale, shaken Nelly Fine interrupted the lesson and asked Celine to go with her. Celine frowned. "We are in the middle of rehearsal, dear Nell."

"I know, and I do apologize." Boh saw the usually upbeat Nell was close to tears. "But this cannot wait. Please, Celine. Grace will be along in a few minutes to finish the class for you."

Boh felt a growing dread in her chest. Celine nodded, and glanced at the class. "Forgive me, ladies and gentlemen."

She left with Nell, and a moment later, Grace, her face tearstained and drawn, reappeared. She closed the door quietly behind her. "Hey, everyone, take a rest, will you?"

They all sat down on the floor, murmuring between themselves. Something was very wrong. Grace took a deep shaky breath in. "Friends ... I'm very sorry to tell you that earlier this afternoon, just after lunch, our dear Madam Vasquez took a fall. No one saw the incident, but we're assuming Eleonor became confused and found her way to the roof."

Boh gasped, as did some of the others, knowing what was coming. Grace nodded, her eyes filled with tears. "Yes. We found her in the alleyway at the side of the building a little over fifteen minutes ago. There was no hope that she would survive the fall, and so we have lost ..."

Grace couldn't carry on and Boh got up to hug her friend as she cried. Most of the others were in tears too. Boh saw Elliott, deathly pale, get shakily to his feet and stagger out of the room. Boh nodded at Jeremy to go find him and Jeremy, his expression shell-shocked, followed Elliott out.

IT WAS hard to know what to do in this circumstance, Boh thought later as they all gathered in the common room. Shocked and subdued, every member of the company gathered with the exception of Nell and of course, Celine. Even when Oona had killed herself last year, Boh couldn't remember such sorrow as this. Liz Secretariat came to find them, her elegant figure bowed by grief.

"Sweethearts, I don't know what to say to you to make you feel better, because there is nothing to say," she said. "Some of you younger ones, Lexie, Keith, you may not know what a legendary prima Eleonor Vasquez was, what a trailblazer."

"We knew, Madam Secretariat," Lexie said softly. "We knew."

Liz squeezed Lexie's hand fondly. "All we can do now is support Celine as best we can, and honor Eleonor's legacy."

"We will do anything we can, work as hard as we can, to do

that, Madam Secretariat," Boh said, still holding Grace's hand. "Anything. Perhaps we should dedicate the showcase to her."

"That's a lovely idea, Boh, and I'm sure Celine will have some ideas of her own. Obviously, that'll be something to discuss after the funeral." She sighed, looking her age for once. "Look, for today, go home, rest. We'll open the studio tomorrow for anyone who wants to dance but I'm cancelling all classes, all rehearsals. If any of you want to talk, or feel you need counseling, please don't hesitate to ask."

Boh's eyes slid to Elliott. Jeremy had brought him back from wherever he'd gone too, but her friend still looked ... devastated? They were all in despair, of course, but there was something different about Elliott's grief.

Later, as they got ready to go home, Boh managed to get him on his own. "You okay?"

He nodded, not meeting her eyes. "Just thinking about Celine, how she must be feeling. To lose your true love ..."

Boh wasn't convinced that Elliott was telling her the whole truth, but she didn't push it. Whatever secrets Elliott was hiding, they were his to hide.

BOH WALKED SLOWLY BACK to Pilot's studio, thinking about what Elliott had said. The thought of losing one's true love ... God, the pain of that, she couldn't even imagine. Unbidden, visions of Pilot, dying or dead, horribly injured, came into her mind and she gave a sob.

Boh moved to the side of a building and let her grief flood out, burying her face in her scarf as she cried. When she was cried out, she wiped her face and started towards Pilot's studio, before stopping and turning around. Running back to the ballet company, she sought out Nell's office. Her friend was sitting at her desk, head in hands, and she looked up as Boh knocked.

"Come in, Boh. Hell, I thought you'd all gone home."

"I was on my way, but I need your help."

Nell looked at her curiously. "What is it?"

Boh drew in a deep breath. "I need an address from you."

BOH WAITED for the building manager to hang up the phone, not knowing what the answer would be. She was surprised when he turned back to her and nodded. "You can go up. Top floor."

She rode the elevator, not knowing exactly what she was going to say, but knowing this was something she had to do.

When she reached the top floor, she knocked on the door of the penthouse apartment. When it was opened, she took another deep breath. "Hello. You know who I am. We need to talk."

"Well, well," Eugenie Radcliffe-Morgan said with a smirk, "Then you'd better come in."

15

CHAPTER FIFTEEN

Months later, Boh would wonder if her visit to Eugenie had done anything but stoke the other's woman's insanity, but for now, she faced the woman who had been her lover's wife for a decade. Eugenie, even thinner when Boh had seen her at Pilot's apartment, her collarbones jutting from the shoulder-less royal blue dress she wore. Boh could tell it was designer and beautifully cut, but it did nothing for the blonde woman, just accentuated her scrawny body, her frailty. Really, she was thinner than some of the more waif-like dancers Boh worked with. Did she ever eat?

Eugenie seemed to be enjoying her scrutiny. "Comparing our bodies to find out what Pilot really likes?" She looked Boh's healthy, athletic body up and down. "Hmm. He usually prefers a more ... slender silhouette."

Boh didn't rise to the bait. For one, she knew that wasn't true, and two, if Boh was confident in one thing, it was that her body was healthy and strong, even with the odd bout of anemia. This woman was deluded if she thought Pilot would prefer a bag of bones.

"Miss Radcliffe-Morgan, I've come here with a request, and a promise."

Eugenie sat down and lit a cigarette. She motioned for Boh to sit, which she did. "I'm listening."

"Let him go," Boh said without hesitation. "Free him, and yourself. He doesn't want you, Eugenie, and I think you know that. So why are you wasting your own time, and his?"

"And yours?"

"And mine. None of us need this constant denial. Pilot and I are together now."

"You're fucking him?"

Boh knew she already knew the answer to that and was just taunting her. "Yes."

Eugenie flicked the ash from her cigarette into an ashtray. "Wonderful cock. So thick and long. Don't you think?"

Boh said nothing. Let her get her coarseness out of the way. Eugenie picked a piece of tobacco from the tip of her tongue and studied Boh. "You're not his type, you know."

"So you've said. The evidence would say otherwise."

Eugenie smirked. "You think you're more than just his latest hole to fuck? He does this with his models. He falls madly in love with them while he's working with them, and then poof! The minute the show is over, he loses interest. Do you really think you could tame that beautiful man?"

Boh didn't believe a word, but she still felt the sting. "Whether or not Pilot and I go the distance is irrelevant. I want you to leave him alone, let him live his life. I know what you did to him."

"What I did to him?" Eugenie sounded incredulously and despite the smile on her face, Boh could see the anger in her eyes. "He drove to me to behave like I never would have if he'd just ..."

"If he'd just what?" Boh's voice was hard. She knew gaslighting when she saw it—her father had been a master of it and now Boh had no patience or empathy for people who behaved like that. "Exactly what you wanted to? Put up with your whoring around? Your drug taking? Yeah, I know all about it, Genie. You treated that …" she cast around for a word good enough to describe Pilot, "that extraordinary man like shit. You took ten years from him. Don't you even feel a little guilty about that?"

Eugenie gave up any pretense of amusement. "Get out. I don't need an ethics lesson from a little mulatto whore like you."

"And there comes the racism. You really are a one-trick pony." Boh got up, wanting to be away from this vile woman as much as Eugenie wanted her out. "Just remember this … I'm on his side. I'll fight for him, with him, against any crap you send our way. Not only that, but I'll talk to anyone who'll listen about how vile and disgusting you are." She stalked towards the door but turned at the last minute. "Here's some free advice, learn how to wipe your nostrils properly, and for the love of God, have a damn sandwich."

Boh slammed the door behind her as she left, knowing that parting shot was bitchy but she didn't care. Eugenie Radcliffe-Morgan was the most revolting person she'd ever had the misfortune to meet. The thought of her hurting Pilot any more … nope. Not going to happen.

Her adrenaline carried her back to Pilot's studio, and when she saw him, looking up from his work and smiling at her, her heart pounded with love.

"Hey, I didn't expect you so early."

His smile faded when she told him about Eleonor Vasquez. "God, I'm so sorry, baby." He put his arms around her and she leaned into his big body.

"I just feel so bad for Celine. Can you imagine, 50 years together and this is how it ends? God." Boh felt the last of her adrenaline leave her body now and she slumped in his arms.

Pilot held her tightly. "There's nothing I can say to make you feel better about this, baby, I'm sorry. But perhaps I can distract you?"

She tilted her head up so he could kiss her. "Please, Pilot, please ..."

His lips crushed against hers and he lifted her into his arms. She stroked his face as he carried her to the couch where they had first made love. Boh smiled up at him. "I love you so much, Pilot, so, so much."

"You're my world," he said as he began to undress her. "My absolute world."

They made love slowly, enjoying every moment of their connection, the rest of the world meting away. As Pilot's cock plunged deeper and deeper into her, Boh trembled and gasped for air, her nipples hard against his chest, her belly quivering with desire as he stroked it. Even when she danced, she could never feel this connected with her own body—he managed to make her feel both precious and unbreakable at the same time.

As they recovered, Boh looked at him shyly and told him how he made her feel. Pilot felt overwhelmed. "Wow. Wow." He shook his head, burying his face in her neck. An idea came to him, as he breathed in the clean scent of her skin. "Baby?"

"Yes, my love?"

"May I take your photograph ... right now? As you lie here, you look so beautiful ... it would be the perfect finale. The way the light is making the sweat on your skin glow gold, your astonishing body ..." He ran his hand down her belly. "You can say no if you want, absolutely no pressure."

"Yes," she whispered, almost as if she couldn't believe she was agreeing to be photographed nude, just after making love. He kissed her gently. "Thank you. I promise, no one has to see them apart from me and you, if that's what you want."

Boh lay, her lithe body stretched out, covered in dewy sweat, and he took the shots, already knowing they would be spectacular. He loved the look in her eyes, sated, loving, sensual. When she looked at him directly with those beautiful brown eyes, he saw trust and devotion in them and it thrilled him. To capture it with his camera was one thing; to know and believe it to be genuine was something else entirely. Boheme Dali loved him as much as he loved her—he had no doubt and the realization almost made him break.

Instead, he concentrated on taking what he knew to be the best photographs of his career. It was a portrait of not just a dancer, but a woman, a girl growing up in front of him, with him. With his gentle persuasion, Boh posed for him, both in dancer mode and casual mode, wrapped in his sweatshirt, grinning up at him, or entirely naked in arabesque, en pointe, or at the barre.

He took closeups of her nude body, the peaks of her nipples, hardened by his touch, the curve of her soft belly with its deep, round navel—the shadows he got using his lights were exquisite.

It became not just a photoshoot, but an extension of their lovemaking, frequently stopping shooting to have sex again, both naked and laughing, playing with every prop they could think of.

It was the early hours of the morning before they stopped and finally dressed to go home. They walked hand in hand through the midnight streets of Manhattan, even though it was cold. "I love this time of night," Boh said, "even in New York, there's a special quiet to it."

Pilot chuckled. "It's weird but I know what you mean."

As soon as he finished speaking, a car backfired and they both laughed. "Jinxed."

"Ha. By the way, with everything, I forgot to tell you."

Boh looked at him curiously. "What?"

Pilot grinned. "The realtor called. The loft is ours."

NEITHER OF THEM spotted the woman following them, watching carefully as they walked back to Pilot's apartment. Her eyes followed them until they disappeared into his building, then she turned and walked away, disappearing back into the night.

CHAPTER SIXTEEN

Grace sat on Boh's single bed and watched her pack her clothes. "I'm going to miss you, boo," she smiled at her friend.

"Me too. I feel kind of bad for leaving you in the lurch like this."

"You're doing nothing of the sort," Grace handed her a stack of scarves. "When you first met Pilot, I kind of guessed this was the way it would go. You just seem so perfect for each other."

Boh grinned. "I know, right? But still, will you be able to manage the rent?"

"Girl, stop worrying. If you can keep a secret, I have news. NYSMBC has offered me a teaching role next season."

Boh stopped. "What?"

"I'm retiring from dancing, at least, for the most part. The stress fracture I suffered last year has made a reappearance and I've had enough." She sighed. "Listen, I made principal at my own ballet company—what else is there?"

"Prima," Boh stressed but then sighed. "But I can't blame you."

Grace studied her. "You getting stressed out about the showcase?"

"Yes and no. I'm concerned because Kristof isn't himself, have you noticed? No temper tantrums, no screaming, no violence. He seems ... subdued, if that isn't too weak a word."

"Maybe he's finally kicked the drugs?"

Boh frowned and Grace chuckled. "Come on, did you really think he had quit? We all know how he fuels himself. How he passes the urine tests, I don't know, but he does it."

"Does the company know?"

"The deal was clean drug tests. He's getting them, which gives Liz and the board plausible deniability. They need him, especially after the anonymous donor. I still wonder who that was, who his benefactor was."

Boh made a noncommittal sound, still thinking about the clean drug tests. Kristof had been calmer, his eyes clearer, his temper restrained. Maybe he was clean, now. She was under no illusion that he wouldn't revert the nearer the showcase got. Two more weeks. She, Vlad, Elliott, and the others had their roles down—it was a waiting game now.

She looked around the bare room. "Wow. If you had told me three months ago ..."

"That you were going to fall in love with a gorgeous billionaire, move to a great loft apartment, and be the subject of a major art installation?"

Grace was grinning as Boh laughed. "When you put it like that." She sat down on the bed next to her friend. "I'll be dancing too. Right at the end of the exhibition, the last photograph will lift and I'll do a short piece. It was Pilot's idea."

"The Arnalds piece?" Grace looked impressed and Boh nodded.

"I took some persuading. Also, I should warn you ... there'll be, um, nudes."

"Of you?"

"No, the Stay Puffed Marshmallow guy. Yes, me."

Grace's eyebrows shot up. "Girl ... I'm so proud of you. Geez, the man has been so good for you. And you for him, I know. He's lost that haunted look he had when we first met him."

"You saw that too?"

Grace tapped her temple. "People watcher. That man was in pain and now he's alive again."

Boh suddenly felt a wave of emotion. "I keep thinking the other shoe is going to drop."

Grace hugged her. "That's just being human, boo, and a New Yorker. We're naturally cynical. Nothing is going to go wrong."

Pilot came to pick her up, and they shared a last meal with Grace, Chinese food which Pilot brought, plus two huge bottles of champagne. He clinked his glass against theirs. "I'd say I feel bad about stealing Boh away from you, Gracie, but I don't," he grinned as Grace laughed.

"Just look after my girl is all I ask."

"I promise, and you know you're always welcome to come stay with us, if you get lonesome. Any time."

Grace smiled. "You really are a sweet man, but as a matter of fact, I already have a roommate lined up."

"She replaces me so quickly." Boh pretended to be shot through the heart, slumping in her chair and letting her tongue loll out of her mouth. Pilot grinned and Grace chuckled.

"Lexie. The kid has to commute from the other side of Paterson every day. I offered her your room at a reduced rate. Hope you don't mind."

"Not at all. That girl hero-worships you, with good reason."

Grace nodded. "I don't know about that, but she's a star in the making."

"No arguments here."

Eventually, Grace threw them out. "Go, go christen your new place, and be happy. I love you both."

As they rode the elevator to their new loft Boh felt a calm descend over her. A new life, she thought, full of love and laughter, and this gorgeous man, holding her hand. She looked up at him, still always surprised by the beauty of his smile.

"Are you okay?"

"More than okay," she said. "I love you."

"I love you too, baby."

He insisted on carrying her over the threshold. She giggled as he pretended to stagger. "We're not married, Pilot; we don't have to do this."

He stopped, put her on her feet, and took her face in his hands. "Yes, we do. This is it, Boheme Dali. The beginning of everything. Our life together. From now on, Boh, we're going to be the happiest people on this earth."

But, of course, he was wrong.

17

CHAPTER SEVENTEEN

Serena slammed her locker shut and made her way down to the outside of the building. Kristof was still teaching class, but he'd given her a key to his apartment. Whether he acknowledged it to himself or not, Serena thought of it as a reward, a thank you, for solving his Eleonor Vasquez problem.

And it had been so easy. The older woman had already been wandering throughout the halls of the company's residency. To lead her up to the roof had been a walk in the park, steering her towards the edge.

"Celine is waiting for you just over that little wall," she'd said to her, and watched as Eleonor Vasquez had walked to her death. Serena told herself that it didn't count as murder.

Kristof had been shocked when she'd told him that Eleonor had died. He had been in bed, sick from weaning himself off the drugs, getting clean. She smirked to herself. Fool. He would never be clean—she was dosing him in his food with a new drug—small doses at first, but enough that she could measure his reaction to them. As she increased the dose, she could see it in his eyes, the slight loss of control again. Good. When she needed him to blow, he would.

She took out her pack of cigarettes as she reached the sidewalk and didn't immediately see the limousine parked at the curb side until the window was slid down.

"Excuse me?"

Serena looked up and saw a thin but beautiful blonde woman smiling at her. "Yes?"

The woman beckoned her closer. "You're Serena Carver, yes?"

"That's right, and you are?"

The woman smiled. "Eugenie Radcliffe-Morgan. I'd like a few moments of your time, if you don't mind. I think we could be of great use to each other."

For the first time, Boh saw Pilot look nervous. Today, they were finalizing the order of his prints in the exhibition, and his friend Grady Mallory was flying over from Seattle to view the photographs.

Despite her bravery in allowing Pilot to photograph her nude, she balked slightly when she saw the huge blow-ups of her body, her breasts, her belly, even the dark triangle between her thighs. They looked stunning, she had to admit, but still, it was her body on display to the world.

Grady Mallory soon put her mind at rest. A handsome blond in his mid-forties, his easy manner and friendly personality eased both her and Pilot's nerves.

"It's incredible, Pilot," he said as they walked around the space at MOMA. "So freaking beautiful. You have gone over and above for the Foundation." He smiled at Boh. "And you ... you ready to be a superstar after this? Because you will be."

She blushed scarlet. "As long as it does the trick for the Foundation."

"And I hear you'll be dancing for us too?"

"If we can get the music cleared," Pilot said, squeezing her hand. "Fingers crossed, but go, I hope so. You should see Boh dance, Grady. It's the second most beautiful sight on Earth."

"Second?" Both Grady and Boh laughed, and Pilot smiled wickedly, nodding at the full-size nude he had taken of Boh just after they made love.

"That's number one."

LATER, one of the assistants at MOMA was talking to Boh about the small stage area where she would dance. Pilot watched her interact easily with the other woman. Grady chuckled, watching him. "Dude, you are in so much trouble. I know that look. You're in love, and you have it bad."

"True story," Pilot chuckled. He and Grady had always been good friends, and Grady, like his other friends, had disliked Eugenie, but had always been too polite to say so.

"Look at these photos. Look at how she's looking at you. Wow, man."

"I know."

Grady nodded. "This is your career high, Scamo, I hope you realize this."

"Believe me, I do. When I met Boh, I met my muse. It almost doesn't matter that she's a ballerina, although it is a fundamental part of who she is. You can't extricate the ballerina in her. But to me, Boh herself is the work of art."

"And it shows in your work, friend." Grady clapped his hand on Boh's shoulder, then smiled as Boh rejoined them. "Can I buy you both dinner?"

Boh looked regretful. "I'm afraid I have rehearsal, but you two should go. I'll see you at home later, baby." She kissed Pilot's cheek, meeting his gaze.

Pilot smiled at her. "Sure we can't drop you off?"

"Nah, the walk will warm me up. Grady, it's lovely to finally meet you. I guess I'll see you at the exhibit?"

"I'll see you in 10 days, lovely lady. My wife, Flori, will be with me. I know you two will get along."

SERENA TOUCHED her champagne class to Eugenie's and smiled. What the other woman had offered her, and what Serena had told her in return, made her realize just how much power she held in her hands. When Eugenie opened her purse and drew out the money, Serena had to fight to keep her countenance. She'd never seen so many 50-dollar bills.

Now, she studied the other woman. "Are you sure? Are you sure you want it to go this far?"

Eugenie smiled. "You can get it done?"

For a moment, Serena hesitated. What she was being asked to do … there was no coming back from it. Yes, the plan meant she would not have to take responsibility to anyone but herself. But could she live with it?

"Carver, I asked you a question. You in?"

Fuck it. "Yes," she said with certainty. "I'm in."

EUGENIE WATCHED THE REDHEAD LEAVE. Ever since she'd followed Kristof home, she'd known he was screwing the younger woman, but it wasn't until she'd actually seen them together that she saw it. Serena Carver had Kristof Mendelev on a string. Kristof! Eugenie had laughed aloud at the thought of it, then almost as quickly, she'd realized how useful that could be in her revenge plan.

Now that Serena had filled her in on the relationship between Kristof and Pilot's little whore, things had gotten a whole lot more interesting, and Eugenie knew she had found a partner, at least for now. The little redhaired dancer had the requisite amount of spite that Eugenie could tap into and she looked forward to working with her.

It also meant she, Eugenie, had a scapegoat and that was always, always a bonus. For her entire marriage, Pilot had been her whipping boy, but now she needed someone else to help punish him.

Genie grabbed her coat. Today called for cocktails at Gibson + Luce on 31st Street. She took the elevator down to the lobby and had the doorman called for a cab. She was still smiling as the driver pulled away from the curb.

SERENA WAITED until Kristof had fallen asleep then went to retrieve the envelope Eugenie Radcliffe-Morgan had given her. She counted the money twice, her hands shaking, and then stared out of the window. Five hundred thousand dollars. Five. Hundred. Thousand. Dollars.

Serena dragged in a few shaky breaths. This was big-time, maybe more than she had contemplated. Could she do this? Should she?

Five hundred thousand dollars.

She heard Kristof stir in the next room and call out for her. She almost felt sorry for him. She looked down at the money again.

Five hundred thousand dollars.

The price of a human life.

CHAPTER EIGHTEEN

Boh's heart sank. She saw Elliott limp into the studio with a resigned look on his face. "Oh, no, El, what happened?"

"Some jerk rode their bike into me this morning, didn't stop."

Boh went over to him. "Is it sprained?"

"I hope to God that's all it is," Elliott said, lowering himself to the floor. He peeled back his leg warmer and they both groaned. Blood was soaking through his legging. "Goddamn it. Maybe it's just a flesh wound. I've danced with worse."

But when Kristof looked at it, he sent Elliott to the hospital. "I want my dancer perfect," he said in annoyance. "Pray, Elliott, that it is only a flesh wound."

But it wasn't. The news came back that Elliott had fractured a metatarsal. He wouldn't be able to dance in the showcase, only a day away now.

"Fuck!" Kristof screamed, making the others silent. Even Jeremy, cocksure that he now would fill in for the injured Elliott in The Lesson, the show-stopping finale of the showcase.

For a few minutes, they all sat in silence. Nell had come to help them discuss what should be done—the tickets had been sold, the audience would expect what was advertised, she said.

"Or better," Kristof said finally, looking between Boh and Nell. "I'll dance Elliott's part."

There was a stunned hush. Nell was the first to recover. "Kristof ... this showcase was supposed to be for the students."

"The student I have trained, religiously, exhaustively was careless enough to get himself injured. I don't trust anyone else to dance with Boh." He waved his hand at Nell. "Make it happen."

Nell looked at Boh who grimaced but shrugged. It was Kristof's showcase; he could dance the whole thing himself if he wanted. Nell sighed and left the room.

"Boh." Kristof clicked his fingers at her, annoying her, but she got up anyway and assumed first position.

AFTER AN AFTERNOON of Kristof's increasingly irritable behavior, she couldn't wait to get home to Pilot. When she opened the door, though, she heard voices. She dumped her bag in the hallway and walked into the living room. Pilot was there, and to Boh's delight, Romana grinned at her, as another older woman she didn't recognize stood up behind Pilot's sister. Romana hugged Boh hard and then whispered in her ear. "It's our mom. Don't worry, but she's about to grill you."

Oh, goodie. As Romana released her, Boh smiled shyly at the older woman. "Hello, Mrs. Scamo ... I mean, Professor Scamo. I'm very glad to meet you."

Blair Scamo smiled, but it didn't reach her eyes and Boh felt her heart sink. Clearly, this meeting was going to be a test of her love for Pilot. Boh's eyes slid to her lover. Pilot moved to Boh's side. "Mom, I think we need to let Boh process this. We—and by that, I mean, you—didn't give her any notice. So, before you launch into Personality Test 101, can we at least have a drink?"

Blair Scamo glared at her son for a moment, then laughed. "Sorry, Boh. Let's start again. Hi, I'm Blair, Pilot and Romana's mother."

"Boheme Dali, Pilot's ... friend." She blushed furiously.

Pilot burst out laughing and Romana rolled her eyes, nudging Boh. "Girl, we just saw the complete collection of Pilot's photos of you. We don't have secrets. Mom knows you two are doing it."

"Anyone ever tell you you're annoying?" Pilot asked his sister, who grinned widely. He kissed Boh's temple. "Babe, why don't you and I go fix some drinks and recover while these two harpies settle in?"

Grateful for the get-out, Boh followed Pilot into the kitchen. "I didn't know they were coming, I swear, and they turned up about five minutes before you. I didn't have time to text you."

"Don't worry about it. Hello," she said, pulling his face down to her for a kiss. He chuckled and pressed his lips to hers.

"Hello, baby. How was your day?"

Boh sighed and rolled her eyes. "A mess. Elliott got injured, badly. Broke a metatarsal."

She grinned at Pilot's blank expression. "Bone in the foot, doofus. Not so good for a ballet dancer."

"Ah. Hey, that sucks. What about—"

"Kristof is taking his place." Boh met Pilot's gaze and knew he was as annoyed as she was.

"The ego of him."

"I know. But he does know the role inside out."

Pilot huffed out a long breath. "I just—damn it."

"What?"

Pilot leaned against the counter and cross his arms. "I know it's acting. I know it's not real ... but I don't know if I can stomach him getting violent with you. Watching it."

She raised her hand to stroke his face. "It is just acting, baby. The one good thing I can say about Kristof Mendelev is that, on stage, he is utterly professional."

"Kristof Mendelev?" Blair Scamo's outraged voice broke through their conversation.

Boh nodded. "He's our artistic director."

Blair looked at Pilot. "You knew about this?"

"Of course. Mom, you know what? Not to defend Mendelev, he's a jerk and an asshole, but he wasn't the one married to me. Genie cheated. I don't like Mendelev but he's Boh's boss."

Blair nodded, and when she looked at Boh, her eyes were sympathetic. "If you can survive being trained by that man, you can survive anything. That's impressive."

"Thank you," Boh said, softly, and looked at Pilot. "Hey, baby, why don't you let me and your mom chat for a while?"

Pilot hesitated then nodded. He kissed Boh's temple again and shot a warning look at his mother.

For a moment, neither said anything. Then Blair grinned. "I think he thinks I'm going to be the Spanish Inquisition."

Boh chuckled. "If you were, I wouldn't blame you. I'm a 22-year-old nobody from nowhere-ville. After what Pilot went through in his marriage, if I were you, I'd be strapping on the lie-detector tests and drugging me with truth serum. Here's the facts. All of this—" she waved her hand around the apartment— "it's great. But I'd live in a paper box with your son. I'd sleep under any bridge in the city as long as he was with me. I don't care about his money. It's his. I love him, the man, that funny, goofy, kindhearted, damaged man in there."

She flushed at her speech but Blair reached out for her and the two women embraced. Boh felt tears in her eyes. "I want to kill her for what she did to him," she whispered.

Blair drew back and wiped Boh's face with her sleeve. "Me too, sweetheart. Me too."

AFTER THAT, they had a wonderful evening with Pilot's mother and sister, and by the end of the evening, they both promised to be there the next evening at her performance.

After they left, Pilot smiled at her. "You made yet another fan. I swear, you're magical."

"Your family is magical. I have to admit, I'm envious."

Pilot held his hand out to her. "Come to bed."

They lay together for a while, talking. "Do you think you'll ever reconcile with your family?"

She shook her head. "No. And, honestly, I know I said I was envious of your family, but that doesn't mean I want my family to miraculously change into them and come back into my life. Too much water has gone under the bridge. Too much."

Pilot stroked her face gently. "For what it's worth ... my family is your family now."

"I love you so much," she whispered, and brushed her lips against his. She couldn't imagine her life without this man now.

He gently rolled her onto her back and moved on top of her. "Is ballet like sports? I mean, the day before a big performance, is it advisable to make love?"

"It isn't just advisable," she said and gasped as, with a grin, he launched his rock-hard cock into her, "it's the law. Especially when making love with the world's best photographer ... oh God, yes, Pilot, like that ..."

He thrust hard and she felt her body responding, her thighs tightening around him as he thrust harder and deeper with every stroke. His eyes were intense on hers as they made love, and Boh felt the love he felt for her. He made her come again and again before they collapsed, exhausted.

Pilot held her in his arms as she drifted to sleep. "Tomorrow, baby," he whispered, "tomorrow you're the star."

"As long as you're there with me, I don't care who the star is."

He chuckled. "Enjoy it, baby. It's your time."

She fell asleep dreaming of applause, of flowers raining down on her, and Pilot, in the audience, proudest of all.

CHAPTER NINETEEN

Eugenie called Serena on the burner phone she had messengered to her. "Is it done?"

"All set. Kristof is the new lead, just like I suggested to him. He'll dance with Boh tomorrow night."

"Good. That's good. And the rest of it?"

"All arranged. They don't expect anything to go wrong, so the security is lax."

Eugenie smiled down the phone. "Are you ready for the shit to hit the fan?"

Serena smiled. "I can't fucking wait."

20

CHAPTER TWENTY

Pilot accompanied Boh to the Metropolitan the next day as they were preparing for the performance. Having him there helped, but she knew Kristof wouldn't like it. So, she gave him a quick tour and ran through the ballets with him.

"At the end of The Lesson, the teacher stabs the pupil to death," she made a stabbing motion to the Psycho music, "and then they carry her body out as another pupil rings the doorbell and the cycle begins again."

Pilot nodded. "So how do you do it? Fake blood?"

"Nah. Takes too long to clean. Believe it or not, I, as the pupil, will just collapse, facing away from the audience, and as the teacher and his housekeeper move the body, they'll drape a red handkerchief over me. It's less gory than it sounds. The horror, really, is the inference that he's done it before, and he'll do it again."

Pilot stroked her cheek. "I can't wait to see you dance, baby."

She grinned and kissed him.

"How very touching, but I need the stage cleared, please." Kristof stalked on, not looking at Pilot. Boh sighed and rolled her eyes at Pilot, who grinned, shooting a death stare at the artistic director's back.

"I'll be watching from the front row, baby. You'll be magnificent, I know it."

Boh kissed him. "I love you."

"Stage clear, now, people." Kristof sounded testy, agitated.

Pilot gave Boh a last smile and left the stage. Kristof finally looked at Boh. "At last. Now, are we going to run this thing through or not?"

Eugenie called Serena on the burner phone she'd sent her. "Everything set?"

Serena chuckled. "Have no fear; it'll all go exactly as we planned." She looked over her shoulder at her erstwhile lover as he barked instructions at the dancers. "He's right on the edge. By the time tonight is over, you and I will both have what we want."

"Good. And listen, I'll be watching. Once it's done, the rest of the money will be delivered to the locker at Penn Station. I appreciate your help—and your silence."

"You can be assured of that," Serena told her smoothly. As long as it helps me to stay silent, bitch, she thought. Despite finding a world in common with the rich woman, Serena did not like or trust Eugenie Radcliffe-Morgan. The woman frightened her, frankly, and Serena didn't scare easily, but there was something, some insanity in Eugenie's eyes that terrified her.

Even Kristof at his most insane didn't have that raw fury, that need for revenge. Did Serena care if people got hurt? No, as long as she wasn't among them. She was in deep now. Killing Eleonor, or at least laying the ground work for Eleonor's "accident" was nothing to her. What would happen tonight excited her. She just didn't know if Eugenie wouldn't sell her out to save her own skin.

Serena put her phone away and watched Boh and Vlad rehearse La Sylphide. She admired the way Boh moved, her extensions long and graceful, her pointe work flawless. To have to follow her on stage was always fraught, trying to live up to the other dancer's prowess.

Serena's eyes flicked to Kristof. He didn't look as amped up as she wanted him to be. She'd slip the rest of the drug into his system just before he went on stage—despite the slight scandal of the artistic director replacing a lead dancer, the chance to see Kristof Mendelev dance had sold out the performance – even the reserve list was packed. Serena smirked to herself. *Tonight, my love, you will have the performance of your life and the whole world will see Kristof Mendelev for the monster you really are.*

Serena watched him for a few minutes more then went to change, ready for her own rehearsal.

BOH WAS TAKING notice of everything Kristof was doing as they approached curtain up. All afternoon, he had been distracted but still barking out insults, his pupils dilated, his skin sweaty. She guessed he was on something, but she was surprised he was letting it show so readily.

She rubbed her wrist. During the last rehearsal of The Lesson, he had been rough with her, rougher than necessary, and at one point, had twisted her wrist so hard she'd cried out. He'd dropped her arm immediately, looking a little shocked himself. He'd muttered an apology and disappeared back to his dressing room, presumably to take a little more of whatever his poison was. No matter. Her wrist was fine, just a little achy, but when she ran through her port de bras, it felt fine.

Despite her concern about Kristof, she felt a calm descend on her. She knew the pieces, knew every move, every step, jump, pirouette. She forgot about the audience who was gathering out front—all except one person. Tonight, she would be dancing for the man she loved, and she wanted to impress and move him with every step.

"Miss Dali? Fifteen minutes, please."

Calm. Breathe in, breathe out. Boh got up and knocked on the adjoining door. Lexie was sitting at her makeup table, and Boh could see the apprentice was trembling. She had been given the role of the housekeeper in The Lesson, a reward for working so hard and impressing Grace, but Boh could see the young girl was terrified. She hugged her.

"Lexie, darling, you will be superb. You'll out-dance both Kristof and myself, so don't be scared." Bo looked around conspiratorially. "Don't say I said this, but there's talk in the ballet company. When you move to the corps, don't expect to be there long. There's talk of a soloist role by the end of next season."

Lexie's eyes grew big. "Are you kidding?"

"No, darling, I swear. The only person who doesn't know you are as good as you are is you."

"Thank you, Boh."

As THE MUSIC BEGAN, Pilot's heart swelled. His sister, seated beside him, nudged him and grinned. Blair Scamo sat on his other side. Any moment now, he would see his love, his adored Boh dancing on this magnificent stage, and for a moment, he didn't know how his heart would be able to cope with it. She had brought him such, joy, such happiness that seeing her in her element ... he couldn't find the words. He looked at his mother, who smiled at him. "You like Boh, right?"

"Darling, that girl is your other half. I can see it, Romana can see it ... Boh is your person and I'm delighted for you both."

Pilot felt his throat get full, and he smiled and nodded, but couldn't speak.

And then the ballet began. As he watched, Boh danced onto the stage, coquettish and flirtatious with Vlad's James, seducing him with her gentleness and ethereal beauty away from his fiancée.

As Boh had promised him, he got lost in the story of it. La Sylphide, a wood spirit, seduced a young man, James, away from his fiancée, and the rejected woman worked with a witch to have her revenge. They were performing Act II of the ballet, where the two lovers were discovered by the wedding party. Pilot watched as Boh and Vlad were convinced by the witch that the scarf she held was a magic scarf that would bind them together.

As the scarf was wrapped around Boh/La Sylphide, she began a movement which played out the tragedy—the scarf was poisoned, and La Sylphide died in James' arms. Pilot felt his chest tighten as Boh acted out her death scene. *They're acting.* Out of the corner of his eye, he saw his mother wiping a tear away.

As James died from a broken heart, the curtain came down to rapturous applause from the audience. Pilot was on his feet as the dancers took their curtain call and Boh winked at him from the stage. Romana whooped, garnering surprised looks from the staid audience, but she didn't care.

Pilot paid little attention to the second part, Romeo and Juliet. Instead he was trying to finalize the arrangement of his photographs in the exhibition. There were so many great shots of Boh that he had an embarrassment of riches to choose from, but he needed to make sure the collection was cohesive.

At interval, Romana chuckled at him. "Dude, did you even see a step of that last part?"

Pilot shrugged. "Not really."

"Thinking about the exhibit?"

He nodded. "I really need to make sure I have captured Boh, not just at rest, but the way she moves, the fluidity ..."

Romana coughed "geek" into her hand and Pilot gave her the finger. His mother was talking to some other guests, and he felt a frisson of excitement go through the room. Romana sensed it too. "Guess everyone's been waiting for this last one."

"Guess so."

As they filed back into the auditorium, he could not help but feel uneasy. Again, he reminded himself that it was just a performance, and he hoped he could keep it together when the ballet got to its most controversial moment.

As the curtain went up, he took in a deep breath and waited.

CHAPTER TWENTY-ONE

Boh knew something was wrong as soon as Kristof made his entrance. His eyes looked wild, unfocused, and angry. She hoped it was just the character, but she knew better. To his credit, though, he played the part perfectly, and Boh was reminded of what a great dancer he once had been.

But as the murder scene approached, she began to feel disturbed. The way he touched her was rough, too rough even for this violent ballet, even for the "Teacher" obsessed with his pupil. As the finale approached, Kristof brought out the prop knife and danced around with it, Boh's character in front of him oblivious to his intentions as he danced behind her.

The moment arrived and Boh turned, seeing the knife for the first time and cringing away as he slashed at her. The knife sliced through the air, then as he brought it back the other way, it skimmed her body, slashing across her stomach.

Oh God, no...

Pain.

Boh jerked away from him, keeping in character, but twisting away. She saw Lexie's eyes open with shock, and then Kristof staring at her. Boh risked a glance down. Blood was spreading across the belly of her costume.

The knife was real.

Boh kept it together—she had to get the knife from Kristof's hand or she was dead, for real. Kristof had frozen, but luckily, Lexie improvised and tore the blade away from him, her character berating him. Thank God for you, Lexie, Boh thought and played out the scene. As she spun around, she saw Pilot was out of his seat, his big eyes terrified, but subtly she shook her head at him. She "died," and then she was being carried off the stage by Lexie and a stunned Kristof.

"Go finish the ballet," she hissed at them, "I'm okay, I'm fine."

How they managed to complete the ballet without breaking, Boh would never know. She quickly grabbed a wrap and put it around herself to go take her final curtain call. She felt the sting of the slash but knew it wasn't deep, that it looked worse than it was.

Kristof was trembling violently, and as they finally left the stage, he fell to his knees, clutching Boh's hand. "I didn't know, I didn't know ..." he kept repeating, almost hysterical, and Boh believed him. Someone else had swapped the fake knife for a real one. Someone wanted her dead.

Liz, Nell, Celine, and Grace gathered around them, Liz calling over the paramedic on duty. She took Boh to her dressing room and made her undress, showing her the wound. Boh winced as the medic cleaned it. It was an eight-inch slash across her belly, but as she'd thought, it wasn't deep. "You might need a couple of stitches in the deeper parts, but otherwise—"

"I honestly feel fine."

They were interrupted by an anxious Pilot bursting into the room. His eyes went immediately to the bloody wound. "Jesus ..."

"Baby, I'm fine, honestly. It's just a flesh wound." She could see he was about to melt down and got up to kiss him. He was shaking so badly she made him sit down, then perched on his knee as the medic smoothed butterfly stitches across her belly. "Sweetheart, breathe."

"What the fuck happened?"

Boh sighed. "Someone switched out the prop knife for a real one."

Pilot gaped at her. "What the actual fuck?"

The door opened and Romana and Grace came into the room. They both looked as shocked as Pilot. "You okay?"

Boh nodded. "I really am. Lexie ... is she okay?"

"Fine. Shaken, but fine. Who would do this?"

Grace's face set. "We don't know for sure ... but no one can find Serena."

They sat in silence for a moment as the implications set in. "Where's Kristof?"

"Believe it or not, he himself called the police. He told Liz and Nell that he had been faking his drug tests, that he believed he had been dosed with something other than coke by someone, and that he deserves to be jailed for what he has done."

Boh gaped at Grace. "You're kidding?"

"No. For what it's worth, I think he's devastated about what happened. He keeps asking how you are."

Boh pulled her leotard up as the medic finish her work. "I want to see him."

"No," Pilot stood up, shaking his head. "No way."

Boh put her hand on his face. "Baby, it's okay, I'm fine. We need to talk to Kristof—he may know something."

Kristof Mendelev was a broken man. What had he become?

He told the police everything as Liz Secretariat listened, then, before they took him to the station for further questioning, he tendered his resignation to Liz.

"I'm sorry," he said, his voice cracking. "I was arrogant and I paid the price. Please, tell Boh I hope she's okay."

"Tell me yourself," Boh said as she came in, flanked by a furious Pilot Scamo. Kristof nodded, relieved that she did indeed look fine as they had told him.

"Boh, I don't know what the hell happened. I screwed up, got loaded, but I swear to you—I did not know that knife was real." He reached out to touch her injured stomach, but Pilot gave a growl and batted his hand away.

"Don't even fucking think about touching her ever again, asshole."

Kristof's shoulders slumped, and Boh put a hand on her lover's arm. "Pilot, it's okay. Kristof, I believe you had no intention to harm me. But we need to know who would, and despite the fact I think we all know who, I want to hear it from you."

Kristof closed his eyes as Liz spoke up. "And I need to know whose urine you were using to pass the tests."

"No," Kristof looked up at Liz, his eyes calm now. "I was the one in the wrong. I virtually blackmailed the person into providing a specimen. I don't want them punished. It's on me."

Liz didn't say anything, her eyes hard. Boh sighed. "Okay, I'll say what everyone is thinking. It was Serena, wasn't it?"

Kristof sighed. "I can't say for sure. But ... if I was drugged with something other than coke, then yes, she is the only one who could have had the access to do it."

"And she hates me." Boh felt dizzy and Pilot steered her into a chair. Boh bent double, dragging oxygen into her lungs. "I just didn't know she hated me enough to want to kill me. God."

"Boh, I'm so sorry." This was a side of Kristof had never seen before. "Look, I'm going to tell the police everything, do what I can to help. I'm not innocent in this, by a long shot, and I'll take what punishment they give me and then some. Liz, I'm sorry. You, Boh, and the company deserve better than me."

After Kristof had been taken away by the police, Pilot took Boh home. Blair and Romana came with them but didn't stay long when they saw the lovers needed time alone.

Romana hugged Boh tightly. "Love you," she whispered. "Get some rest."

After Pilot kissed them goodbye, he closed the door, locked it, then came to her, wrapping his arms around her. "Are you sure you're okay?"

"I'm good." She leaned into his warmth. "I wouldn't mind a soak in the tub. Come join me?"

Pilot brushed his lips against hers. "Just try and stop me."

As they soaked in the warm water, Pilot washed her hair for her, massaging the conditioner into her long dark hair as she lay against his chest.

"In all of the confusion," he said softly, "I didn't tell you how beautifully you danced. I was blown away."

Boh sat up, turning to smile at him. "You liked it?"

"Do you even need to ask? You're a goddess, Boheme Dali, both on the stage and off it."

She smiled and took his hand, pressing it against her left breast. "You have my heart, Pilot Scamo. Tonight I danced for you and you alone."

They kissed, lips firm against the others and Pilot's mouth curved up in a smile. "Boh?"

"Yes, baby," she murmured against his lips and Pilot chuckled.

"If we don't rinse your hair now, you're going to be stuck with the conditioner in your hair because there's no way that in a few moments we're not going to be fucking."

"Hah, convoluted grammar, but okay then."

Quickly rinsing her hair, she straddled him. "Touch me, Scamo."

His hand slid between her legs and began to massage her clit and she moaned, pressing her lips against his neck. Pilot slid two fingers into her cunt, seeking her G-spot, and she ground her sex against his hand.

Her own hands reached down to stroke his cock, so thick and heavy against her hand, her fingertip tracing a line over the sensitive tip, making Pilot shiver with pleasure. His free hand fisted her hair at the nape of her neck and pulled her face down to his so he could kiss her, his tongue massaging hers. "I want to be inside you, woman."

Boh grinned and they shifted so she could take his cock deep inside her, sighing happily as he filled her. They moved slowly, the bath water slopping around them as they moved. Pilot sucked on her nipples as they fucked and Boh closed her eyes, giving herself over to the sweet pleasure of it all.

LATER, in bed, Pilot drew her close, his arms curving protectively around her. Boh closed her eyes but couldn't sleep, too amped up by everything that had happened. Such a close call. He owed Lexie big-time for getting that knife from Kristof, but she truly didn't believe Kristof meant to hurt her, no matter how high he was. Which left Serena. Boh was still in shock about the fact that Serena could go as far as wanting to kill her. Jealousy was a powerful thing.

. . .

Across the city, Eugenie listened to Serena's excuses of how Boheme Dali was still alive and felt nothing but rage. "You stupid little bitch ... you assured me this would work."

"I did everything I was supposed to—and now I need you to come through. I have to get out of the city."

"Not my problem."

Serena hissed. "I could go to the police and tell them everything, don't forget that, you stuck-up piece of crap. I'm sure your ex-husband would love to know you tried to kill his lover."

Eugenie snorted. "The only thing wrong with that is that he'll know that if I wanted her dead, she would be dead. This is why I shouldn't work with amateurs. I'll deal with it myself."

"And me?"

Eugenie smiled. "If I were you, Miss Carver, I'd get out of town before either the police or I catch up with you."

Hearing the click on the other end of the phone, Serena smiled. The call was recorded on her phone now. Mutually assured destruction, she thought. Serena had taken as much money from her account as possible and grabbed what she could to sell from Kristof's apartment all in preparation days ago, but there was no way she was going to leave town without bringing everyone else down with her.

She stuck her phone in her pocket and drained the last of her coffee. She pushed her way out of the coffeehouse into the night and stood at the crosswalk.

She never saw the car which aimed straight for her and took her out before coming to a stop. Serena was crushed under the front wheels as people around her started to scream. The driver got out and retrieved Serena's phone from her. As she gasped for life, her chest crushed, her right leg almost severed by the huge SUV, the driver frisked her then got back into the car without saying a word and sped off.

As Serena bled out, her last living thought was that Eugenie's psychosis far outranked any she had ever known, and that somewhere deep inside, she felt sorry for Boh and Pilot, knowing they would never have a moment's peace while Eugenie Ratcliffe-Morgan was alive.

CHAPTER TWENTY-TWO

"Dead?"

The detective nodded. "At the scene. A hit and run as far as we know. We're interviewing witnesses." He looked at Boh sympathetically. "I know you would have rather Miss Carver faced legal justice."

Boh nodded. "I would never have wished her dead."

Pilot, next to her, made a noise. "In all honesty—good riddance. I doubt anyone will mourn for her."

Boh knew he was angry, but she squeezed his hand. "It's over now." She looked at the detective. He had come to see them at the ballet company, where Boh and Pilot had been asked to attend a meeting with the company's leadership. Liz, Celine, Nell, and even the founder, Oliver Fortuna, a stately Englishman in his late seventies, sat listening in silence now as the detective broke the news of Serena's death.

The detective bid them goodbye. "Any further information, we will, of course, let you know."

LIZ TOLD them all that the board had appointed Grace as the

new artistic director of the ballet company, effective immediately. "We need stability now, after everything. Kristof's showcase was very well received, but we would be naive to think that what happened won't hit the newspapers. Randall McIntosh is already sniffing around. He noticed something, despite you and Lexie doing an excellent job of covering up." Liz smiled at Boh. "Given the circumstances, you were a warrior, Boh. How are you feeling?"

"Honestly? Kind of numb. Physically, fine, really. Lexie ..."

"She's fine, shaken. We gave her the rest of the week off, but still, she's in the studio with Grace this morning."

Boh smiled. "That's our girl." She looked shyly at Oliver Fortuna. "Mr. Fortuna, Lexie is an exceptional dancer, and her work ethic is second to none. I hope we can take that into consideration when discussing her future with our company."

Oliver smiled. "You can bet we will, Boh." He looked at Pilot. "Nell has shown me some of the work you have been doing—sensational. We'd like to keep working with you, if you have the time and the capacity."

Pilot nodded gratefully. "Thank you. I'm honored by that."

"We're all looking forward to your exhibition on Friday. And, personally speaking," Oliver continued, "I'd like to make a contribution to the Quilla Chen Foundation. Now, before you get excited, I'm thinking we could hold performances which benefit the Foundation ... believe it or not, I'm not cash rich."

"Any contribution would help, thank you." Pilot looked at Liz. "But I understand some of the ballet's financiers are getting skittish?"

Liz sighed. "What with Oona's suicide, Eleonor's accident—my apologies, Celine—and now this ..."

Pilot nodded. "Liz, Oliver ... the Scamo family will make sure that you never, ever have to worry about funding for this company. We will make up any shortfall and contribute extra if required."

Both Oliver and Liz looked stunned. Nell smiled at her old friend. "I might have known."

"What do you want in return?"

Pilot looked surprised at Oliver's question. "Nothing. Apart from ... treating your dancers well. That's all I ask." He squeezed Boh's hand.

PILOT SAT with Boh as she changed into her leotard and shoes. The changing room was empty—Saturday morning, most of the dancers had the day off. They had passed the studio where Grace and Lexie were rehearsing—or rather, gossiping—and spent a few moments with their friends.

"I know I should use this time to rest," Boh said, "but I really want to dance. Just for an hour or two. Practice the piece for your exhibition." She tapped his camera. "You can use this or just watch, if you like."

"I do like."

He sat against the mirror. Boh realized she always felt calmer when he was near, when he was watching her. She had someone to whom she could channel the passion that she felt when she danced. As the beautiful music played, she used Pilot's handsome face as her focus, her body curving toward him, yearning, loving.

When she finished, he applauded her, and she could see how moved he was. She went to sit next to him and he kissed her. She grinned and ruffled his curls. "Pretty boy."

Pilot laughed. "Lunatic. Boh, Jesus, it's a privilege to watch you dance."

She leaned against him. "It's an honor to know you, Pilot Scamo. You bring out the best in me."

"We do that for each other, I think."

"You're right."

There was a knock at the door and Elliott, pale and wan, stuck his head in the door. Boh and Pilot scrambled to their feet. "Hey, El, come on in."

Still on crutches, he hobbled in. "Can I talk to you both? It's important."

AN HOUR later they were back in Liz's office. This time Celine was the one who looked pale. After Elliott told them the story of how Eleonor had caught him and Kristof in the bathroom, he explained how Kristof told him that Serena had known and had offered to "fix" the problem. The shock of learning Eleonor's death wasn't accidental was palpable, but Celine nodded.

"I did wonder if someone led her up to the roof. It wasn't one of her normal routes she took when she was confused. I honestly believed no one would want to hurt my love ... but now we know Serena Carver was a psychopath." She looked at Boh. "Thank God she didn't succeed a second time."

Pilot was on edge. Boh could sense the tension in his body, but when he spoke, his voice was calm. "What I don't get is how someone like that could exist in this environment, where everything is shared. People walk around exposed, physically and mentally, and no one saw the madness in her? What about her family?"

"Estranged."

Pilot sighed. "Celine, I'm so sorry for your loss. I just want to understand why Eleonor died and why Boh was nearly murdered last night."

"I think we all do." Liz said. "But now that Serena is dead, we'll never know. We have to move forward." She looked at

Elliott, whose shoulders slumped down. "And I need to talk to Elliott alone for a few minutes."

Boh squeezed Elliott's shoulder as they left the room, then she and Pilot walked home to their apartment.

"So much damage," she said, and Pilot nodded.

"We'll get through this, baby."

She smiled at him. "I know. I love you."

He stroked the back of his hand down her face. "As I love you. Come on. Let's have lunch, then maybe you can help me at work."

"Love to."

THE GOOD THING about being filthy, stinking rich, Eugenie thought, was that one could afford a fleet of private detectives to stalk one's ex-husband and know what he was doing every second of every day.

Now, as her detective streamed his video, she watched Pilot and his dancing girl walking to his studio—the studio he thought Genie knew nothing about. The Carver girl, now thankfully silenced—what an amateur—had failed in her mission to kill Boheme Dali, so now Eugenie had to step up.

And, by God, did she know how she was going to do that. This time next week, two more lives would be destroyed, but hers would be the happiest it had ever been.

She couldn't wait.

23

CHAPTER TWENTY-THREE

Grady Mallory introduced Boh to his wife, Flori, and two friend who had accompanied them. "Boh, Pilot, these are Maceo and Ori Bartoli. Pilot, Maceo is interested in showing this exhibition in Italy. Discuss." Grady finished with a grin as Maceo and Pilot laughed, shaking hands.

Flori bore Boh and Ori away to get drinks. "This is the boring part. Listen, I know Quilla will be here soon, so let's get a head start on drinking."

Boh giggled. The two women were a lot of fun, but Boh's attention was always being drawn back to her lover, being feted by his peers, the press, art critics. The had exhibition opened an hour ago, and Boh had just about gotten used to her most intimate parts being on display for the public.

She had to admit, Pilot had photographed her nude in such a way that it wasn't exploitative at all. Most people were commenting on the love in her eyes and she knew Pilot was pleased. It truly was a collaboration between her and him—Pilot might not be in the photographs, per se, but he was right there with her in every shot.

There was one shot of them, a small shot for Pilot's biography at the end of the exhibition. Both of them were laughing, foreheads touching, so much love between them. Boh had made Pilot promise not to sell that shot.

"I have the original on my computer," he'd laughed at her but he'd promised.

"I just don't want anyone else to have that shot. It's us. It's everything we have been through together."

Pilot had already had some offers from people, but he wanted to wait until he'd shown the exhibition around the world. Boh knew Maceo Bartoli was big in the European art world, the equivalent to the Mallorys in the States, and that a world tour would be the shot of confidence that Pilot needed right now.

And she would be by his side for every single moment.

QUILLA CHEN MALLORY was a staggeringly beautiful woman, Boh decided, and one of the loveliest people she'd ever met. When the head of the foundation arrived with her husband Jakob, she walked around the entire exhibition, arm in arm with Boh, and talked to them both about each photograph in detail. Boh watched her greet both Ori and Floriana with hugs—obviously old friends—but she still included Boh in their conversations. She introduced them to her friends from the ballet, and soon Boh felt as if she had known them for years.

Quilla, her lovely almond eyes twinkling, took Boh to one side. "Sweetheart, these photographs are astonishing. I do hope that you and Pilot continue to collaborate. I've never seen him so fired up. I don't mind telling you, Grady and I were a little concerned that he'd lost his mojo over the last few years."

"I think that was mainly the stuff going on in his private life."

Quilla nodded, her smile fading. "Yes. I had the misfortune to meet Eugenie a few times. Vile woman. I could never figure out what he saw in her." She squeezed Boh's hand. "But he has the right woman now."

She looked at the audience, all seemingly entranced by the photographs on display. "It seems to be a success."

"And then some," Grady said, coming up behind then with a beaming Pilot. "I've already heard from the critic from the Times—major awards were mentioned. Congratulations, man. Both of you."

Pilot put his arms around Boh, burying his face in her hair. "Thank you," he whispered, his voice full of emotion. "This is all because of you."

Boh shook her head. "No, baby, this is your night."

"Our night," he insisted and she chuckled.

"Okay, our night." She checked her watch. "Almost time to dance. I'd better go get ready."

"I'll come with you."

Boh grinned, knowing exactly what he had in mind and as they escaped to her dressing room, Pilot locked the door and took her in his arms. Boh grinned at him as he kissed her. "Feeling frisky, Mr. Scamo?"

"You know it."

They made love quickly in the cramped dressing room, laughing and celebrating as they did. "God, I love you, Boheme Dali."

"You are my world, baby. My entire world."

They tidied themselves up and Boh changed into her costume, a beautiful floating dress, made for her by Arden at the Company. It had layers of light silk which would float around her body as she danced, in various shades of blue and gray.

They walked hand in hand to the little stage and waited for Pilot to be announced by Quilla. He would make a short speech and then introduce Boh's dance.

Quilla spoke for a few minutes, then, with a huge round of applause, Pilot walked on stage.

"Thank you, thank you. I'm overwhelmed by your kind words, and by your presence tonight. I have to be honest. I never thought I'd show again. The last couple of years, I doubted myself, my passion, even my will to carry on. That all changed six weeks ago when I met the woman in the photographs. In Boheme Dali, I found inspiration, confidence, life, and love. We truly are a partnership, something I've never had before. It is Boh who should take all the plaudits here, and I'm delighted to say she's agreed to dance for us. I know that you will fall in love with her, as I have done. Ladies and gentlemen, Boheme Dali, prima ballerina."

Boh's eyes were full of tears as she walked on to the stage. "I love you," she said to Pilot, who grinned and kissed her cheek.

"Knock 'em dead, baby. I love you."

He left the stage and Boh took her position. She felt no nerves as she began to dance, her mind completely on translating her feelings for Pilot into dance. Her body felt as light as air as she danced and when she was finished, it took her a few seconds to hear the rapturous applause from the audience.

"Wow," Quilla said, coming back onto the stage and hugging Boh. "That was so beautiful, Boh, thank you. Incredible."

Pilot came on to take Boh's hand and they walked back to the dressing room, unable to stop staring at each other. As Boh changed back into her dress, Pilot took her hands.

"Marry me," he said simply, his eyes full of emotion. "I never, ever thought I'd say that to anyone ever again. I was determined not to. But finding you, Boh ... I know it's crazy fast, and if you say no, I swear, there's no pressure ..."

"Dude, chill," Boh said, her voice shaking, grinning at the repeated moment from when he'd asked her to move in with him, "Chill." Her voice broke. "Yes," she said, tears dropping down her cheeks, "yes, Pilot Scamo, I'll marry you. Of course, I'll marry you!"

He picked her up and twirled her around, whooping loudly as they both broke into delighted laughter. Finally, he put her down. "You have truly made me the happiest man on Earth."

"Me too. I mean, the happiest woman. I haven't got a secret dong." Boh was giggling now and Pilot laughed.

"You sure?"

"I am. I definitely haven't got a wing-wang."

Pilot threw back his head and laughed. "No, you doofus, are you sure you want to marry this old man?"

"Not so old. And yes. God, yes, just try and stop me."

"Ha, I won't even try. We're engaged."

Boh kissed him and they began to walk back to the party. "How grownup of us."

"Isn't it?"

Back at the party, they told Blair and Romana about their engagement and both were delighted. "Thank God," Blair said, kissing Boh's cheek. "I was hoping he'd lock you down."

They all laughed, and Romana playfully punched her brother's arm. "Hey, I forgot to give you this earlier. A little gift for your evening." She handed him a small package and he opened it to reveal a pocket square. On the corner, stitched beautifully, was the word: Loser.

Pilot busted out laughing as Romana grinned. "Thanks, sis." He tucked it into the pocket of his suit, making sure the embroidered word was showing. Boh grinned, shaking her head. "What kind of insane family am I marrying into?"

Blair pretended to be insulted, then smiled at Boh. "Too late now, you've said yes. Come on, let's go grab some more champagne. It's a special night."

. . .

THE PARTY WENT LATE into the night, and Boh found herself talking to everyone who seemed to come. They congratulated her on both the pictures and her dancing and by one a.m., her head was whirling. Quilla came to find her to bid her goodbye. "I left Jakob at the hotel looking after the kids and they've had way too much sugar." She hugged Boh. "Next time you get to Seattle, or we come here, promise me we'll have dinner and catch up."

"I promise."

Boh wanted to find Pilot and tell him that she had a girl crush on Quilla, knowing it would make him laugh, but she couldn't find him. She asked Grady where her lover was.

"He just had to go back to the studio and pick up some provenances the gallery asked for. No biggie. He tried to find you but asked me to tell you he'd be right back."

"Oh, okay, thanks, Grady."

Grady nodded to the exhibit. "This will put him over the top, you know. We've had calls from galleries all over the world. Maceo has already locked him down to show in Venice and Rome."

"It's what he deserves," Boh said fondly and Grady clinked his glass against hers.

"Amen, sister."

An hour later, and Boh still couldn't find Pilot. She tried his cell phone but it went straight to voicemail. Blair and Romana came to say goodbye and found Boh frowning. "Is everything okay?"

"I can't find Pilot." She explained where he had gone.

Romana chewed her lip. "I'm sure he's around so—" She trailed off and looked past Boh's shoulder, out of the window of the gallery.

Both Blair and Boh turned to see Eugenie standing outside, staring in at them. There was a cruel twist to her smile as she gazed directly at Boh and Boh felt her pulse quicken. What the hell?

"Miss Dali? This was just sent for you." A gallery assistant held out a padded envelope to her and Boh took it. She pulled it open and reached in, feeling something sticky. She pulled it out and gasped. Blood. A blood-soaked piece of cotton. As her heart pounded heavily against her chest, she turned it over and read the single word embroidered onto it.

Loser.

No. God, no. She looked up to see Eugenie smirk at her, then turn and disappear into the night.

"No, no, no, please, no ..." Boh began to run. "Call 911," she screamed back at a stunned Blair and Romana. "Send them to Pilot's studio!"

Then she was out in the night, running through the city, ignoring the strange stares she was getting from passersby. She ran the few blocks to the studio and burst in. "Pilot!"

She searched the studio, knowing what she was about to find, but when she did, she knew she could never be prepared. Pilot lay on his stomach, his arms flailed out at his sides, his eyes closed. Despite the black color of his suit, she could see the blood, the stab wounds in his upper back. She dropped to his side and tried to turn him over. He was lying in a pool of blood and at first, she couldn't tell where he had been stabbed. She listened for his breath, trying to still her own gasps of horror. He was breathing—barely.

"Baby, please hold on, please, please ..." She heard sirens coming closer and a minute later, Romana, Blair, and Grady burst into the room as Boh tried desperately to keep the blood inside her lover's body.

She looked up at them, tears pouring down her face. "She stabbed him ... she stabbed him ... no, no, please, Pilot, don't go, stay with me ... stay with me ..."

CHAPTER TWENTY-FOUR

Hollow.

That was how Boh felt as they waited in the relatives room of the hospital. She'd seen the loaded glances of the paramedics as they fought to save Pilot's life—it didn't look good.

When they'd opened his shirt, Boh had seen the stab wounds in his chest. Too near his heart. Eugenie had been merciless. The police were looking for the blonde socialite now, after both Boh and Blair had told them they had no doubt that Eugenie had done this. She'd planned it all—the call to the gallery to ask for the provenances, knowing Pilot wouldn't send someone else, knowing he would go collect them himself. She'd waited for him, then attacked him. His arms and hands were covered in cuts, defensive wounds, but Eugenie had had the element of surprise.

Boh couldn't stop picturing it, the knife sinking into Pilot's back, then, as he fell, that demon woman on top of him, stabbing him over and over.

God, please, Pilot ... please, fight. Fight.

Romana, her usual exuberance gone, her face pale, suddenly turned up the television.

"A night of triumph and terror for world-renowned photographer Pilot Scamo. After the triumph of his new show, Boh, by Scamo, the 40-year-old now lies in hospital, fighting for his life after being stabbed in his studio. Although police have yet to confirm it, it is rumored that Mr. Scamo's ex-wife, Eugenie Radcliffe-Morgan is a person of interest in this horrific crime. The attack comes a week after Mr. Scamo's muse and rumored lover, ballet dancer Boheme Dali, was reportedly injured after during a performance."

"Turn it off, please." Boh put her head in her hands as she heard Romana click the television off. She felt Blair put her arms around her.

"He'll be okay. My boy knows how to fight." But she didn't sound convinced. Boh hugged her back tightly.

"Give me five minutes with that bitch and I'll make sure she never hurts anyone again." Romana was furious and hurting, Boh knew. She tried to smile at her almost-sister-in-law.

"Join the queue," she said.

They sat waiting for hours, then finally, a surgeon came to see them. Although he had changed, there was a smear of blood on his scrubs, dark red, and Boh couldn't take her eyes off it. His blood. Pilot's blood. Oh God ...

"We've stabilized him, but there will be a long recovery—if he makes it through the next few days. The knife penetrated his heart, but we think we've managed to repair it. He's fighting, which is good, but I expect him to remain unconscious for a few days." He sat down next to them. "That's a good thing—it gives his body the chance to recover. He's in good condition, the right weight for his age, and obviously fit. It's all positive, but we should still take pause. His injuries are serious, and he remains a critical patient."

"Can we see him?"

The doctor patted Boh's hand. "Would you be upset if I asked you to wait until he's out of recovery? An hour or two, then you can all sit with him."

"Thank you, doctor." Bair nodded at him and Romana shook his hand.

THE THREE WOMEN were allowed to see Pilot an hour and a half later, and Blair and Romana sat one side while Boh sat on the other, holding his hand. He was so still, his dark curls flat against his skin, usually so olive and swarthy, now pale and drained. Dark violet shadows were under his eyes. Boh bent down and kissed his cool lips. "I love you," she whispered, "please come back to me."

AFTER TWO DAYS, Blair made Boh go home to shower and sleep. "I'll call you the moment anything happens," she promised as she firmly steered Boh into a cab.

At home, Boh felt the silence ringing through their apartment. The emptiness she felt inside overwhelmed her and she broke down, curling up on the floor of the living room and sobbing all her pain out. As her sobs finally quieted, she fell into an uneasy, exhausted sleep.

Waking a couple of hours later, she dragged her aching body into the shower and stood under the hot water for long minutes. She'd barely eaten since Pilot's stabbing, and now she felt the need to eat something. Pilot would need her to be strong for him for months now.

She checked her voicemails, listening to all of her friends calling to check in, asking after Pilot, telling her how sorry they were. She'd call them back later—it would distract her from watching over Pilot. God. It was hell watching him, unable to talk to him, knowing that he was in such pain. She wanted to take all that pain into herself and save him from it.

Her cell phone rang as she was scarfing down scrambled eggs and she grabbed it, hoping to see either Blair or Ramona's name.

"Miss Dali?"

"Yes?"

"Jack Grissom here, detective with the NYPD." It was the detective who had shown up at the crime scene—he had been kind and polite.

"Hi ..." Her heart began to beat quickly. "Detective, tell me there's good news."

"We have her. We have Eugenie Radcliffe-Morgan."

The relief was overwhelming and Boh tried to stop her hands from shaking. "Does she admit to stabbing Pilot?"

"She's lawyered up and isn't talking at all—but her hands are covered in cuts. She's guilty as hell. We stopped her from flying out of the country. Her private plane was waiting at Teterboro. She was arrogant enough that she thought we wouldn't be watching." He sounded as angry as Boh felt.

"I want to talk to her."

"I can't allow that, I'm afraid, not while she's being questioned. We'll charge her and transfer to a holding jail. You can see her there but I can't guarantee she'll agree to meeting you."

"Will she get bail?"

"Not if I can help it. She's already proved a flight risk and the nature of her crimes ... we believe she also arranged the murder of Serena Carver. We've proved they were working together."

Realization dawned. "I'm not surprised." She talked a little longer to the detective then thanked him.

Boh walked around the apartment, her mind whirling. Did she actually want to see that bitch? No. All she wanted to do was get her hands around Eugenie's throat and squeeze the life out of her ... no. Unlike you, Genie, she thought, I couldn't kill another person, not even you.

Boh jumped as someone pounded at her door and as she yanked it open, she saw Romana, hot and breathless from running. Boh's heart failed. Romana grabbed her hand.

"You have to come now," she said, breathing hard, "he's awake."

CHAPTER TWENTY-FIVE

Pilot saw her face and it was like a shot of pure morphine through his aching body. "Hey, pretty girl."

Boh's face was wet with tears as she kissed him. "Pilot, Pilot ..." she seemed to choke on her words and she began to cry.

"Hey, hey, hey, I'm okay." The tubes in his arms stopped him from reaching out to her, but he managed to stroke her head. "It's okay, baby, really."

Boh got herself together, clutching his hands. "Sorry, baby ... how do you feel?"

"A little groggy, but actually fine. I assume that's the drugs." He grinned at her. "God, you're even more beautiful than when I saw you last."

"That is the drugs," she chuckled, wiping her face. She stroked his hair back from his forehead, her smile fading. "Pilot ... was it her? Was it Eugenie?"

He nodded. "Yeah. Why didn't I see that coming?"

"None of us did. They've arrested her, and are pretty sure she's guilty, that they'll get a conviction. She'll try and bargain for a plea deal but the detective says they're going to throw the book at her."

Pilot nodded. "Okay. Good." He sighed. "Maybe we can finally believe that it's all over?"

"I hope so, baby."

Pilot beckoned her down so he could kiss her lips. "The minute I get out of here, I'm marrying you, Boheme Dali. I cannot wait a minute more to begin our life together."

"Neither can I ... and I have something I need to tell you."

Pilot searched her eyes. "What is it?"

Boh had tears in her eyes. "I don't know how it happened, we've always used a condom ... but I'm pregnant."

Pilot's answering smile stretched across his handsome face. "My God ... talk about meant to be."

"I know. When I took the test this morning, I couldn't believe it, but now ... it's a sign, Pilot."

"I love you so much, Boheme, and I can't wait for our little slugger to be born."

Boh started to laugh and cry at the same time. "Six weeks. Six weeks and our lives are so different. And despite everything ... I'm so happy, Pilot. Please, get well fast ..."

Pilot reached out for her and she went into his arms, gingerly, not wanting to hurt him. "From now on," he said, as his lips found hers again, "from now on, Boh, everything will be good."

"Promise?"

He smiled at her. "I promise ..." and he kissed her again, knowing this was the first moment of the rest of their lives ...

THE END.

SIGN UP TO RECEIVE FREE BOOKS

Sign Up to Receive Free E-Books and Audiobook Codes.

Would you like to read **The Unexpected Nanny, Dirty Little Virgin** and **other romance books** for **free**?

You can sign up to receive these free e-books and audiobooks by typing this link into your browser:

https://www.steamyromance.info/free-books-and-audiobooks-hot-and-steamy/

Or this one:

https://www.steamyromance.info/the-unexpected-nanny-free/

PREVIEW OF WHILE YOU WERE GONE

A Christmas Second Chance Romance

By Michelle Love

Blurb

Young Manhattan editor Maia's life falls apart two days before Christmas when her husband and daughter go missing. Desperate to find them, she is devastated when her husband's car is found next to a notorious suicide bridge with a note that simply reads "I'm sorry."

For the next five years, Maia struggles to come to terms with the tragic loss. Finally she begins her life over, moving across the country to Washington state and opening a local book shop on one of the islands in Elliott Bay.

She begins rebuilding her life, but when she meets enigmatic architect Atom Harcourt, they begin an erotic, passionate love affair, and Maia finally finds happiness.

Soon a series of troubling incidents lead Maia to believe someone is targeting her, and as the five-year anniversary of her family's disappearance looms, malevolent forces surround her, and she doesn't know who to trust.

Will Maia ever find the answers she is looking for? And who is the mysterious stranger lurking in the shadows... and is he a stranger at all?

This is a romantic suspense novel perfect for the holidays with no cliffhanger, plenty of steamy sex scenes, the purest love, and of course—a guaranteed happy ever after!

This novel contains characters from another of my books, *Evergreen*. Check that out for Emory and Dante's love story...

At an exclusive Manhattan party, two days before Christmas, renowned architect and property magnate Atom Harcourt meets the most beautiful woman he has ever seen, and although they spend less than a minute talking, he realizes that none of the sexual relationships he has been indulging in mean anything because the connection he feels to this mysterious beauty shocks the hell out of him.

Five years later, he relocates back to his hometown of Seattle to build a friend's new home and is staggered when he meets the mysterious woman again.

Maia Gahanna is still recovering from the trauma of her husband killing both himself and their small daughter five years earlier but when she meets Atom... she remembers him—remembers the spark between them. Tired and feeling sad, she makes a brave decision and soon they become lovers.

But then Atom is stunned when Maia is almost killed by two seemingly unconnected incidents and when it becomes clear it wasn't random at all, he is terrified of losing the woman he loves.

Will Atom and Maia's love story end tragically or will they become stronger together through adversity?

This steamy, erotic story has no cheating and a guaranteed HEA, but will still thrill you with both new and old characters from previous stories (*Evergreen*) and a central love story which will have your heart both ache and soar as Maia and Atom fight for their love.

~

Two days before Christmas, New York tech billionaire Zach Konta leaves his Upper East Side home in Manhattan and waves goodbye to his beautiful, much younger wife, Maia. A loving father, Zach is smiling and blowing kisses as he and their five-year-old daughter, Luka, leave to go Christmas shopping for Maia's gifts.

They never return home.

Five years later, after learning that the police are no longer investigating the disappearance and are assuming Zach and Luka are dead, Maia realizes she has to move on with her life. But rumor and suspicion dog her every move, her old friends have drifted away, and eventually she leaves New York and her old life behind to start again on a small coastal island in Washington state. Opening a small bookstore in the little town, Maia soon finds herself warming to her new home and to the new friends she meets there and hopes to leave the terrible grief of her past behind.

Enigmatic architect Atom Harcourt has his own demons to battle. Reeling from the sudden death of his father, a man never satisfied with his son's successes, Atom is looking for anonymity and solitude. When a friend commissions him to build a private home on the island, he hopes to blend in, but he quickly attracts the attention of the island's female population.

But Atom isn't looking for romance. Instead, pursuing commitment-free hookups, he goes to anonymous sex clubs and sleeps with beautiful women whose names he doesn't bother to learn. But then he meets the most beautiful woman he has ever seen, and his heart begins to yearn for something he has never had—a soulmate.

Soon Atom and Maia are falling hard for each other, and both have to decide whether they can trust enough to make a relationship work. After a few missteps, they begin to build a life together but then a series of weird occurrences begin to destroy Maia's peace of mind.

Maia's world is turned upside down as she begins to think that her daughter might be alive—as well as her ex-husband—and it soon becomes clear that someone is trying to hurt her and destroy her new life. Maia and Atom fight to find out the truth before the killer finally comes for Maia, and Atom loses the love of his life... forever.

CHAPTER ONE

Maia rolled over onto her stomach and pretended she didn't see her five-year-old daughter creeping into her parents' bedroom. Luka, her long dark hair, so like her mother's, messy and tangled, clouded around her sweet, chubby face as she tried not to giggle.

Maia waited until Luka climbed up onto the end of the bed and was creeping towards the pillows before she reared up, roaring, making her daughter scream and laugh as Maia tickled her.

Maia finally relented and scooped Luka up into her arms, blowing raspberries on her cheeks then nuzzling her nose against her daughter's. "Good morning, Nugget."

Luka giggled, wriggling so she could lock her arms around Maia's neck. "How many sleeps now, Momma?"

Maia grinned. "Seven, sweetie." It was a week before Christmas, and Luka had been nagging at her parents to get a tree and decorate it. "Almost everyone else has already had theirs up for weeks, Momma."

"I know, sweetie, but you know what Daddy's like. He says it spoils it if we celebrate too soon."

But today, a week before Christmas, she and Luka had the

whole day planned out. The tree was being delivered to their Upper East Side apartment later that morning, and they had already shopped for way too many ornaments and fairy lights. Luka was almost beside herself with excitement.

Maia got herself and Luka showered and dressed for the day before heading to their kitchen. Their cook, Joelle, smiled at them. "Today's the day, huh?"

While Luka ate her breakfast, Maia checked her messages. Zachary, a proven workaholic, was already at work, but he'd found the time to send her a message despite being the CEO of a multi-national tech company.

Hi darling, have a wonderful day with Nugget today. I love you. Z

Maia smiled to herself. Many people had told her they thought maybe Zach was too aloof for her fun-loving nature, or he seemed distant when they were at parties, but Maia knew that her husband of six years was merely shy. When they were alone, they sincerely enjoyed each other's company, and Maia thought he reined in some of her wilder tendencies.

Maia Gahanna met Zachary Konta when the elusive tech billionaire arrived at her prestigious Manhattan publishing house to discuss his biography.

Maia, then a subeditor of non-fiction, had attended that meeting, shadowing her boss and mentor, Eliza Pentland. She hadn't expected to contribute much, but the moment Zach Konta had stepped into the room, his eyes had settled on Maia and never left.

Maia had been uncomfortable with his scrutiny, especially when her boss Eliza seemed pissed at her. She deliberately didn't speak to Konta, but an hour after he left her boardroom, a vast bouquet of flowers arrived for her with a note.

Dinner? I'm not the kind of man who takes no for an answer.

Maia had raised an eyebrow at that. Well, there's always a

first time for everything, Mr. Konta. She had been all set to call him and refuse his invitation, but Eliza had spotted the bouquet and read the note before Maia could stop her.

Maia told her boss she was refusing the date, and to her surprise, Eliza shook her head. "No, keep it. Maia, we need this book deal with him."

Maia had been shocked, and Eliza held up her hands. "I don't mean sleep with him! Of course not, but a working dinner... he was obviously taken with you, and as a client, he could be valuable to this company."

There was an implied threat in her words—*come through for me or your job could be at risk*—and so, reluctantly, Maia agreed to have dinner with Konta.

MAIA SMILED TO HERSELF NOW. She hadn't stood a chance. Zachary Konta was handsome, charming, and attentive. That first dinner turned into a second and a third, and within three months they were married. Now, seven years on, Maia still felt the whiplash from Zach's full-on love bombing.

Maia had grown up in a children's home on Long Island and had been through a number of foster homes before finally striking out on her own. By working three jobs and getting bogged down with student loans, she'd put herself through college, even gaining a scholarship to Columbia, and by hustling and interning, had landed herself a junior editorship at Pentland and Cops Publishing House.

Eliza had been a thorough but fair mentor, but she and Maia were never close. Her aloof exterior did warm, though, after Maia's marriage. Eliza recognized the potential of being in Zachary Konta's social circle.

Always good-natured and generous, Maia accepted her new position in society with ease and grace and didn't care that Eliza was using her to improve her own situation. It didn't have any effect on the happiness Maia felt with Zach.

He was twenty years her senior, forty-eight to her twenty-eight, and they celebrated their seventh wedding anniversary a month ago. Their greatest joy in life, though, was undoubtedly Luka. Their precocious, loving daughter had brought them closer together.

THE ONLY DARK cloud on their seemingly perfect lives was Zach's health. A year ago, he'd been diagnosed with a mild depression, and sometimes, the black moods took him to a place that scared his wife. He would become withdrawn, irritable, and a little possessive of Maia. She weathered his moods with love and patience, and eventually he would emerge, apologetic and remorseful.

Today, she and Luka would go shopping for gifts for him. When they were first married, she was at a loss to know what to buy the billionaire husband who could afford anything, obviously, but soon she learned all he wanted was her company and that of Luka's.

Zach, liked her, loved to read, and so when Luka was bundled up against the December cold, they went to their favorite bookstore to find something for his gift. Gerry, the bookstore owner, greeted them with a smile. "Maia, you're in luck. I've just come back from antiquing in Connecticut, and you'll never guess what I found."

He rummaged around the cash register and pulled out a book, handing it to her. Maia smoothed the leather cover. *Solaris* by Stanislaw Lem. One of Zach's favorite authors. She smiled up at Gerry. "Really?"

"First edition, too. I thought of you immediately."

"This is perfect, Gerry. Thank you. Nugget, why don't you try to find something you would like as a treat while I talk to Gerry?"

Luka smiled and wandered over to the children's section. Gerry's bookstore was a small, independent place with oiled wood shelving and books that weren't just from the *New York Times Bestseller List*. Maia and Luka could spend hours in the store, and Gerry was so laid back, he never minded. With the store so small, he and Maia could chat while keeping an eye on Luka.

Maia paid for the Lem book and Luka's treat, and they waved goodbye to Gerry, wishing him a happy holiday. They held hands, swinging them gently as they walked to the different stores. After an hour of strolling, Maia took Luka to a coffee shop and bought her some hot chocolate.

Her phone rang as she was served with her tea, and Maia smiled gratefully at the waitress. "Hello?"

"Hello darling, it's me."

Maia smothered a grin. Who else? "Hey honey."

"I just wanted to remind you about the party tonight."

"I remembered, sweetheart. Nugget and I are going to go find me some shoes soon."

Zach chuckled. "Any excuse."

Maia frowned a little. What was that supposed to mean? She was hardly a spendthrift. "Well, you know I always want to look my best for you."

"I meant nothing by that, sweetie. Sorry, I was distracted for a moment. And you could turn up in a garbage bag and still be the most beautiful woman in the room."

"Ha," Maia flushed at the compliment, her anger forgotten, "Have you been drinking? This early, Mr. Konta?"

Zach laughed. "It's true, regardless. Anyway, I was just checking in. That's my excuse to talk to you. Is Nugget enjoying shopping?"

Maia handed the phone to her daughter. "Dadda wants to say hello."

She listened, smiling, to the conversation Luka had with her father. She was still smiling when Luka handed the phone back.

"See? How we're going to get her to sleep for the next week, I don't know. Do people still disapprove of drugging your kids?" She crossed her eyes at Luka to show she was kidding, making her daughter giggle.

Zach laughed. "I think it might be frowned upon. Look, baby, I have to go. I'll see you later, okay? I love you."

"Love you, too."

THEY SHOPPED for another hour or so, then went home. Maia had taken some time off from the office for the holidays, having been a workaholic throughout her pregnancy and Luka's formative years. She regretted that now, but at the time, she had wanted to prove to the world and to herself that she was a modern woman—that she could do it. Mostly, she had to admit, she had wanted to prove to those people in Zach's social circle that she wasn't a gold digger, that she had her own agency, that Zach wasn't her sugar daddy. *Ugh,* she hated that saying.

In the last store, she sought out the assistant's help as she tried on shoes for the party. Maia loathed wearing heels, but knew flats were a no-no, so she enlisted help to find some heels that were semi-comfortable at least. Luka played with the empty shoe boxes and helped the assistant sort them back into the right ones before getting bored and wandering off to look at the sparkly kids shoes.

Maia, who hated shopping for shoes, was losing the will to live, and the assistant grinned at her. "You hate this."

"Yup."

"I would, too... well, look, what color is your outfit?"

Maia smiled. "Midnight blue."

They went through a few options while Maia had one eye on Luka. The assistant brought out a final option, and Maia's eyebrows shot up. "Wow, really?"

The assistant held out a pair of what Maia could only describe as Dorothy's ruby slippers. She grinned at Maia. "It's Christmas. Plus, who doesn't need some glitter in their lives?"

The shoes were gorgeous, but not quite fitting for the Upper East Side—but what the hell, Maia thought with a chuckle. "I'll take them."

She glanced over at the children's section—and her heart failed. Her daughter was nowhere to be seen.

Luka was gone.

CHAPTER TWO

"Luka?" She darted over and looked around, panic building. "Luka, honey?" Her voice was rising. "Sweetheart, don't hide now..."

The assistant came over, a concerned look on her face. "Is everything okay?"

Terrified now, Maia looked at her, her eyes wild. "My daughter..."

"Momma!"

Maia whirled around to see Luka jump out from behind a pillar, Zach grinning behind her. Maia's heart began to slow, but now she was annoyed. "Don't *ever* do that," she said, glaring more at her husband than her daughter. She saw Luka's face drop and hurriedly bent down to her height. "Sweetheart, it's just I was worried."

"Daddy said it would be fun." Luka looked between her mother and father uncertainly.

"Don't worry, sweetie, Momma's just being silly. It was a prank, Maia, that's all."

Maia glared at Zach, her anger simmering. What the hell

was wrong with him? Did he think he was funny? And what the hell was he doing here?

Biting her tongue, she returned to the cashier and paid for her shoes, and the family left to go home. Luka was subdued now, and Maia knew she had picked up on the tension between her parents.

To distract her daughter, Maia suggested they go to Rockefeller Center and see the tree there, and that seemed to work. Maia picked up her daughter and hugged her tightly, trying to hide how annoyed she was with Zach. She didn't speak to him directly the entire time.

At home, Luka went to play in her room, and Maia and Zach went to change for the party that evening.

After a few moments of tense silence, Zach sighed. "Maia... come on. It was just a dumb prank."

"Making me think I'd lost my daughter, Zach? That's not a prank, it's just... cruel. Why on earth..." Maia's voice was rising. Was she being too hard on him? Had it really just been a thoughtless joke? "Don't *ever* do it again."

"Believe me, I won't." Zach muttered, stalking into the bathroom.

Great, Maia thought, still annoyed. *Now we'll have an entire evening of snarking and tension.* She was still pissed—did Zach think an apology was beneath him?

She changed into her dress and did her makeup while Zach was in the shower, then went to find Luka. The little girl was laying in her book nook, reading one of her favorite stories. Not caring about her dress, Maia crawled inside with her and kissed her. "You okay, Nugget?"

Luka nodded, but Maia could see the wariness in her eyes. "Look, darling, it's okay. Daddy just didn't know I'd be so upset, but you know, it's only because the thought of losing you, of never seeing you again, would break my heart, you know? I love you so, so much, Nugget, more than anything in this world. Don't be sad. Sometimes people do things that they think might be funny, but really, they're not. Daddy made a mistake is all. It's okay."

"Momma... are you and Daddy going to split up?"

"No! Gosh, Luka, no... sometimes people have arguments, but they don't last. I love Daddy and he loves both of us. No biggie, okay?"

"No biggie?"

"No biggie." Maia kissed Luka's cute button nose. "Sarah will be here soon, and she called me earlier and told me she's bringing some crafts for you two to do together. So, you can stay up a little later than normal, okay? For a treat."

Luka's eyes lit up. "Okay."

WHEN MAIA CRAWLED BACK out of the book nook, her heart felt eased. Zach was waiting for her, smiling. He helped her to her feet and drew her close. "I'm sorry, Maia. I was an idiot."

He kissed her gently, and she felt the last of her anger slip away. "You're forgiven."

His kiss grew deeper. "I love you, Mrs. Konta."

She chuckled. "Right back at you, Mr. Konta."

They went back to their bedroom to finish dressing and to Maia's surprise, Zach loved her sparkly Dorothy shoes. "That'll show those stuck-up bitches. You look beautiful, darling."

And for once, she felt beautiful. Maia checked her reflection one last time. Her caramel skin, inherited from her Indian mother and Creole father, glowed with the light makeup she had put on, and her long dark hair fell in soft waves down her back. The midnight-blue dress clung to her full breasts, flat stomach, and curvy hips. She wasn't the tallest woman—only five-foot-four—but the heels gave her an extra inch or so next to

Zach's six feet. He was gloriously elegant in a dark blue suit, and he took her hand as they said goodbye to Luka and Sarah the sitter and went down to the waiting limousine.

MAIA UNCONSCIOUSLY STRAIGHTENED her spine as they walked into the party. Even though she knew these people well, she still felt like an outsider. She hadn't been born into this world; she had married into it, and she suspected many of Zach's contemporaries looked down at her. There was one woman, in particular, who repeatedly made it clear that Maia didn't belong and never had. Tracey Golding-Hamm, a stick-thin blonde socialite, beautiful in a pinched, snooty way, had always harbored a crush on Zach and when he'd married the decidedly non-snooty Maia, Tracey hadn't even attempted to hide her disdain. Maia wasn't scared of her; she just hated being in the same room as the vicious blonde.

The couple throwing the party, however, were two people she did like and respect. Henry Klein was Zach's college roommate and business partner, and his wife, Sakata, was a charity maven who actually did more than just throw parties for show. Sakata and Maia had hit it off immediately; as Sakata put it, they were the 'Asian contingent'. Maia had laughed at her description and nodded. "We represent, all right."

Sakata also had no time for the bitchier members of their circle, those men and women who looked down on Maia when she married Zach. "Girl, you have two college degrees, and you're a major force at your publishing company. And you did it on your own. Those jerks have never had to try."

Maia spotted Tracey making a beeline for her and Zach and excused herself. The mood she was in, she didn't want anything to do with the vile bitch.

Coming to her rescue, Sakata bore Maia off as soon as they

joined the party. "Come with me; I know where Henry's hidden the good booze."

She and Maia retreated to the kitchen and found a bottle of scotch. Sakata waved it triumphantly. "Henry will kill me but who cares? I have to put up with his crappy taste in wine."

Sakata and Henry enjoyed a rambunctious relationship, forever play-fighting and fooling around. Henry was so easy going and Sakata so mischievous that they seemed incongruous in this world, but Maia wished her own husband was a little more like Henry, fun-loving and chilled out.

But then again... she told Sakata about Zach's prank. "Am I overreacting?"

Sakata pulled a face. "No way. What a jerk move."

Maia felt a little better. "Right? I wanted to kill him."

"I would have certainly made sure I kneed him somewhere painful."

Maia snorted with laughter. "Damn, never thought of that."

Sakata speared an olive from a platter waiting to be taken into the party and popped it in her mouth. "Not like Zachary to play pranks."

"I know. Maybe that's why it shocked me." Maia took a slug of scotch and grimaced. "Ugh."

Sakata snorted. "Yup. Best to sip that one. How did Zach know you were in that store?"

"He said he was just passing and saw us."

"Random."

Maia nodded. She wasn't sure if she believed Zach's story either, but she had no reason to believe otherwise. He was hardly the type of person to keep tabs on her, but a small chill went up her spine anyway. *Don't be stupid... this is Zach we're talking about—the man you love, the father of your child. You know him better than you know yourself.*

She decided to change the subject. "So, who's coming

tonight? Apart from the Witch Queen of Angmar. I've already seen her."

"The usual, both good and bad." Sakata grinned. "Oh, and a few new people. A couple we met when we were in Jakarta for the conference, Julia and Gordon VanDusen. She's lovely, but he's... well, sweet but grabby so keep your eyes open and duck away when you can. And someone Henry's trying to schmooze, Atom Harcourt."

"Name rings a bell."

"You've probably heard of his father, Alan Harcourt, the property magnate. Atom works for him." Sakata lowered her voice. "He's *gorgeous*, absolutely to die for, but very closed off and reserved. He brought a date but seems to be content to ignore her and drink on his own. I don't think Henry's going to get very far with him."

Maia already felt a kinship with the newcomer. "I wish I had the balls to go hide out. No offense, but you know how much I hate parties."

"No offense taken. For my work, it's a necessary evil." Sakata studied her. "Talking of work... I hear Eliza might be moving on."

Maia flushed. No one was supposed to know about her impending promotion to editor-in-chief—not even Zach knew. But Sakata had spies in many camps. "Nothing is set in stone yet, so I'm not getting excited about it. I don't want to jinx it."

Sakata squeezed her arm. "It's very well deserved, honey, but my lips are sealed, I promise." She sighed. "Well, let's go and rejoin the party. I'll point out the hunk if he comes out of hiding."

Maia was still giggling when they went back to find their husbands. Zach snaked an arm around Maia's waist. "You look happy."

"Always with you," she said and kissed his cheek. He leaned

his forehead against hers.

"Does this mean I'm forgiven?"

Maia smiled. "You're forgiven... and when we get home tonight, I'll show you just how forgiven you are."

His eyebrows shot up and desire glowed in his eyes. "I'll make you keep that promise, Maia Konta."

To Maia's relief, the party was a laid-back affair, and the more aloof people kept to themselves. Sakata introduced Maia to Julia and Gordon, and Maia was delighted to see a mischievous glint in Julia's eyes. Gordon was a little boorish but friendly nonetheless, and Maia warmed to the new couple, inviting them for drinks after the holidays.

"I would love that," Julia confided, leaning in conspiratorially. "Some of these women look—"

"—terrifying?" Maia grinned at her new friend and Julia laughed.

"Yup."

Maia chatted easily with Julia while Zach and Gordon talked business and before they knew it, people were starting to leave. "Is it that late already?"

Maia looked around for Zach who had excused himself while she was occupied. "Excuse me, Julia."

"Good to meet you! Call me after Christmas, promise?"

Maia kissed her cheek. "I promise." She liked the other woman immensely. They chatted for a while, then Henry came to claim his wife to introduce her to some other people.

Maia turned and almost groaned out loud. Tracey was right next to her. "Hello, Maia." She looked her up and down, smirking when she saw her red glittery shoes. "Are we going for Las Vegas Hooker-style? I had no idea this party was fancy dress."

"Sure you did or you wouldn't have come as a raging bitch." Maia shot back. "You might want to mix up your costumes. That one's getting pretty old." She downed the last of her champagne, gave Tracey her most insincere smile and walked away. *Yes. Got her.* It was petty, but Goddamn, it was satisfying.

She wandered through the remaining people, trying to find her husband. When she couldn't find him, she went out to the balcony for some air. It was bitterly cold, and she shivered but the fresh, sharp air cleared her head.

"Are you looking for someone?"

Maia whirled around at the sound of his voice. Behind her, a man stood up from one of the balcony chairs. He was tall, easily six-five, and broad-shouldered. His dark brown hair was all loose curls, his eyes a vivid green. Three days of dark scruff defined his utterly perfect face.

Maia was aware she was staring but she couldn't help herself. He was the most beautiful man she had ever seen. He half-smiled at her scrutiny. "Believe me, this—" he pointed at his face, "—is a curse, not a blessing."

His eyes were steady on hers, and he reached out and touched her cheek. "An exquisite woman like you must be taken."

Maia swallowed hard and nodded. "I'm looking for my husband."

The man smiled. "*Husband.* Just my luck."

"Maia?"

She heard Zach's voice behind her and rearranged her expression into a smile. "Hey, darling, I was looking for you. This is—" She turned but the beautiful man had disappeared. "A wonderful view." She finished awkwardly, nodding to the view over Central Park.

"Nothing compared to what I'm looking at. Let's go home, darling."

CHAPTER THREE

Zach was so loving and attentive on the way home that Maia forgot about the beautiful man, and by the time they had said goodbye to the sitter and checked on a sleeping Luka, she was tired.

But Zach was already hard for her and he peeled her dress from the shoulders. "Keep the shoes on," he murmured, his lips against her throat.

Maia chuckled, then gasped as he ripped her panties from her and deftly unhooked her bra.

"Christ, you're so gorgeous, my love…" He laid her back on the bed and pushed her legs apart. He unzipped his pants and drew out his already hard cock.

"Do you want me to suck you, baby?" The fact that he was still in his suit while she was naked and exposed was turning Maia on, but Zach shook his head, instead pulling her legs around his waist and thrusting into her. She gasped at the quick violence of it, but soon they found their rhythm and made love, Maia pulling at Zach's clothes, her lips hungry on his.

. . .

SHE WOKE in the middle of the night to find the bed empty beside her. She sighed. This had happened a few times over the last few months—Zach was finding it difficult to sleep. She slipped from the bed and padded silently through the apartment to find him. He was sitting in his study, his headphones on, staring out of the window.

Maia slipped her arms around his shoulders and hugged him. He lifted his headphones off, setting them on the desk, taking her hand and drawing her onto his lap. She stroked his face, noting the dark circles under his eyes. "What is it, my love?"

Zach shook his head, holding her close, and she stroked his hair. "Is it me? Am I upsetting you in some way?"

"No, darling. You and Luka are the best things in my world. I'm just feeling..." He gave a choked laugh. "I can't even put it into words. Unsettled. Frustrated."

"With what?"

He shrugged. "Life. I don't think depression has a reason, Maia—it just comes. My mother used to suffer from it, too."

Maia held him close. "You've never told me much about your parents."

"I suppose I haven't."

Maia waited, but he didn't go on. She pressed her lips to his. "Come back to bed, darling. I can help relax you."

His hand slid up her thigh underneath her nightgown. "Why not right here?" He said, his voice ragged with arousal. Maia grinned and straddled him as he pushed her nightgown up over her hips.

Maia freed his cock from his sweatpants, and he guided himself into her, pulling down the strap of her gown and exposing her breast as they made love. He took her nipple into his mouth, sucking on it hard and making her gasp and shiver with pleasure. She rode him hard, moaning his name over and over until they both came.

Zach let her lead him back to bed afterward, and she wrapped herself around him, cradling his head against her breasts.

But when she slept, she dreamed of vivid green eyes and a sad smile.

Maia drew her daughter's coat around her. "Keep this buttoned up, Nugget, because it's really cold out there."

Luka nodded, smiling. "It's snowing."

"It is. A white Christmas, how about that?" Maia pulled Luka's favorite hat onto her silky, dark hair. "Now, are you both sure you don't need me to come with you?"

Zach grinned and Luka protested. "No, Momma. How are we supposed to buy you surprises when you're there?"

"I'm just kidding, Nugget." She kissed Luka's plump little cheek. "Be good for your Daddy."

Zach swung Luka up into his arms and kissed Maia. "We'll be fine."

"See you later." She followed them to the door and smiled at them. "Have fun."

Zach stepped into the elevator but then stopped. "Have a happy day, Maia."

She grinned. "Without you two? I'll try but I can't promise anything."

She waved to them as the doors closed, then went back into the apartment. She had some work to catch up on, but really, she wanted to wrap all of Luka's gifts before they got back. Even when they thought Luka was asleep, they did not dare risk wrapping her gifts in the evening time—Maia swore blind that Luka could sniff out a gift from a mile away,

Outside the snow was falling thick with the Manhattan

skyline wreathed in clouds, and the light was dim. Maia flicked on the Christmas tree lights and spread paper, tape and bows around her. She turned on *Miracle on 34th Street* on the huge flat screen television and spent a contented morning wrapping presents, watching the movie, and drinking warm spiced apple juice.

When the gifts were wrapped, she checked the clock. Three p.m. They had given their staff—really only their chef, Patricia, and their cleaner, Hannah—paid vacation time, and although Maia loved the two women, she was happy that she had the apartment to herself. She would make supper for them all: Luka's favorite of meatballs and spaghetti (in truth, it was her own favorite, too) and an apple pie. On Christmas Day, she would cook a turkey, but for now, she set about chopping vegetables and seasoning ground beef and pork for the meatballs.

Finally, she slid the dish into the oven to bake in the tomato sauce and checked the time again, frowning slightly. It was almost six, and she had expected them home before now. She checked her phone—no message. Hesitating slightly, she dialed Zach's number. It went straight to voicemail.

"Hey, honey, if you get this, can you give me a call? Just wondering when I should expect you? Guess you two are having fun, huh? Love you. Give Nugget a kiss from me."

She clicked off and put the phone down on the counter. She expected it to ring straight away, but it stayed silent. *Don't panic, everything is fine... it's fine.*

She went to draw a bath, thinking it would distract her, but as she lay in the warm water, her phone on the bath next to her, she found she couldn't take her eyes off of it, willing it to ring.

There's nothing to worry about; they're probably just caught up in the fun of it.

But by seven, out of the bath and dressed in her robe, Maia began to feel panic rising. She went through the stores that Zach was likely to go to for her gifts. The bookstore, Chanel,

Bergdorf's... hating herself, she went to his desk to see if she could find any clues. *Any moment, they'll walk through the door and laugh at me for being so worried... any moment.*

She saw an appointment written down on his blotter for one of the more exclusive perfumeries in the city and, taking a deep breath, she called it and explained that her husband had an appointment.

"Yes," the woman on the phone told her, "but I'm afraid Mr. Konta failed to show up for the allotted time." The woman sounded a little pissed, but Maia didn't care. Her heart was cold and frozen. Zach never missed appointments. Without explaining, she hung up on the woman and dialed every one of the stores she would expect Zach to have visited, even the odd random stores they'd only ever been to once.

None of them had seen him. "He would have had our daughter with him," Maia said, desperate now, "A cute kid with a red coat and a blue woolen hat with a pink star on it?"

"I'm sorry, ma'am, but we have thousands and thousands of customers today. It *is* Christmas Eve."

That was the answer she got from all the stores, and even the smaller stores couldn't help her. She tried Zach's phone again and then called Sakata. She explained why she was calling, trying to keep the panic out of her voice, but Sakata was immediately concerned. "We're coming over. Have you called the police yet?"

"Not yet."

"Do it. We'll be over as soon as we can."

Maia bent double in her chair, trying to pull oxygen into her lungs, trying to quell the panic. This wasn't happening, this wasn't happening. Any moment, Luka would come running into the apartment, calling for her, wrapping her little arms around Maia's neck...

She called the police who were polite but disinterested until she told them who Zach was. Then, miraculously, they got real interested real quick. "We'll send someone over at once, ma'am."

Maia shook her head, smiling grimly. She'd be outraged at their favoritism, but right now, she'd take it. Anything to find Luka. And Zach, of course...

If this was another of his 'pranks'... it was way, *way* too far. But the cold hand squeezing her heart told her this was no prank, no sick joke.

Sakata and Henry arrived just as two detectives appeared at her door, and Maia went through her worries with them and what she'd done to try to find her husband and daughter. To their credit, they assured her that they would follow every lead.

"Aren't we supposed to wait twenty-four hours?" What was she saying? Maia felt her composure slipping. She wanted to scream at them to go, go find her child and her husband, but that came out instead.

Sakata put her arms around Maia as she started to sob, and Maia heard Henry talk quietly to the two detectives. "Look, obviously, this is very worrying for Maia."

"It's okay, sir. Ma'am, when a minor child is involved, we don't wait the twenty-four hours."

"Thank you, thank you, please, she's just a little girl." Maia wasn't sure if they could understand her through her sobs, but the detective nodded.

"We'll stay in touch, don't worry."

THE NIGHT CLOSED in and there was no word. Maia redialed Zach's phone a hundred times, but soon the voicemail was full, and she was talking to dead air.

Eventually Sakata called a doctor and although Maia protested, she eventually let him give her a sedative. It didn't knock her out though, but she lay on her bed, her ears straining for any news, ready to hear Luka's sweet voice calling for her.

BUT THERE WAS NOTHING. As dawn broke, Sakata brought her hot tea. Maia sipped it gratefully. "You've gone over and above for me," she told her friend. "I can't ask you to stay."

"You can, and anyway, I'm not leaving. Henry's gone out to search everywhere he can think of."

"He has?" Maia felt a rush of gratitude. She held Sakata's hand. "Do you think—"

"No. They're fine. There's a perfectly reasonable explanation for this. You'll see…" Sakata's voice broke a little, and she looked away. It made Maia's heart constrict; Sakata knew, like her, that this wasn't good. This wasn't normal.

It was Christmas Day. Maia got out of bed and went into the living room. Seeing Luka's gifts under the tree made her falter, her whole body shaking. "Oh God…" She sank to her knees. "She's gone, isn't she?"

Sakata came to her, and they wept together, Sakata unable to give her friend false hope, and Maia was strangely grateful for it. She didn't want to hope, didn't want the pain of believing her daughter would be returned to her safe and well, because if it didn't happen…

It was unimaginable, but it was happening right now. Luka and Zach were missing.

HOURS STRETCHED INTO DAYS. New Year's came and went, and the world went on around Maia as if her whole life hadn't been ripped apart. She'd sent Sakata and Henry home at last, grateful for their love and support but told them she couldn't ask any more of them.

She had no one else to turn to. Her colleagues, her friends, all of them offered but Maia wanted to be alone—alone so she could scream, alone so she could go out walking in the middle of the night searching everywhere she could think of for any sign of Luka and Zach without anyone stopping her.

One of the things she and Zach had bonded over was that neither of them had a family. Maia had been given up at birth by her mother and had gone through the foster care system. Zach's parents had died in a car wreck when he was seventeen, leaving him a vast fortune but alone in the world. Any other relatives had drifted away when they discovered he wouldn't share the money with their deadbeat asses. It had been one of their greatest regrets that Luka didn't have grandparents, especially when she started kindergarten and came home in tears, asking them why every other child did.

Maia went into her daughter's room now and lay down, burying her face in the pillow, breathing in the powdery sweet scent of Luka's hair. The pain in Maia's soul was searing, burning hot as hell. She couldn't believe she would never see her precious Luka again, nor her husband...

THREE DAYS LATER, the police came to see her and told her they'd found Zach's car abandoned at the side of a bridge on the Cornell University Campus, his alma mater. Inside the car was Luka's backpack and a note to Maia simply saying, "I'm sorry."

There was no sedative the doctor could give Maia that had any chance of containing her raw, desiccating grief at the finality of it.

Luka and Zach were gone.

CHAPTER FOUR

F*ive Years Later...*
Seattle

ATOM HARCOURT NODDED as the judge granted his divorce. He didn't look at Gail as she stood across the room from him. He already knew what her expression would be. Pain, betrayal, hatred. And he deserved it all. Gail was a good woman, and he'd been selfish enough to marry her just to make his father happy. It hadn't worked.

Now his father was gone, and Gail loathed the very sight of him. *I'm sorry,* he wanted to tell her, *I'm sorry I'm such a weak bastard.*

He risked a look at her. Her elegant, patrician features were blank as she stared back at him, but her eyes told him the story of her sadness and pain.

God, I'm sorry...

He stepped towards her as the judge dismissed the court, but

Gail turned her head and stalked out, ignoring him. He knew she would never talk to him again, and he didn't blame her.

Atom thanked his lawyer and left quickly, slipping into his Mercedes and driving out of the city. He kept driving in no particular direction until he reached the coastline, then, ignoring the fact he was wearing a seventeen-thousand-dollar handmade suit, he walked along the beach for miles. Even when it started to rain he didn't turn back, grateful that the bad weather meant he was alone.

And he *was* alone. In the week since his father had died, Atom had been in denial, but now he knew it was the case. His mother had died when he was a kid, and his older brother disappeared into the Australian interior years before and didn't keep in touch. For years it had been Atom and his father, locked in some kind of twisted power play between father and son, always trying to one-up each other.

And Atom was tired of it. His father's death had released something inside of him, a freedom... a kind of relief. The guilt that brought was almost unbearable.

What a fucked-up life. Atom slowed down, breathing hard. He might be wealthy beyond reason, handsome as Adonis, but that was nothing to Atom. He wanted...

What did he want? Marriage clearly wasn't for him. He spent his twenties and thirties fucking his way around the world's most beautiful women, but that hadn't made him happy. He'd been seeking someone who didn't exist. A soulmate.

Only once had he felt the promise of something more—a brief moment at a party five years ago. A moment on a cold December night at an acquaintance's' party.

Her eyes, those large deep brown eyes, wreathed with dark lashes. Her sweet smile. God, it had been less than a minute, but she'd haunted his dreams ever since.

Stupidly. She was married for Chrissakes. After the party,

Atom had flown back to Seattle and tried to forget her, but now and again her face would fill his dreams.

Lately, in an effort to assuage his loneliness, he'd begun to frequent sex clubs, the more exclusive ones deep in the city. Anonymous and discreet, he indulged in as much sex as he wanted, without ever having to know the name of the woman he was fucking.

He preferred it that way.

Atom rubbed his face now. Christ, he was so messed up. Something had to change in his life. Something had to give him purpose.

HE DROVE BACK to his apartment in the city. In the shower, he held his face up to the cool spray, hoping to clear his head. He was meeting an old friend this evening, Dante Harper, who'd just moved back to the city with his wife Emory. The couple had spent a few years in Dante's mother's home country of Italy but were now back in Seattle. Atom and Dante had been close friends as children, and now Atom felt a wave of hope. Dante had always been a steadying force in his life—maybe he could confide in his friend and seek guidance.

Something had to change, that much Atom knew. He just didn't know what to do to change it.

"ATOM!" Dante hugged his old friend tightly, and Atom felt his heart lift. Dante introduced him to the lovely woman at his side. "Atom, this is my Emory."

Atom kissed her cheek. "So, it's you who's made this old man so happy? Good to meet you at last."

Emory Harper smiled at him. "And you, Atom. Dante talks about you all the time."

She was beautiful, and Atom felt a pang. Her caramel skin, her large dark eyes... she reminded him of the girl on the balcony.

Over dinner, he learned that the couple had a daughter. "She's eight now and a handful," Emory laughed, showing him a picture of a young girl with merry, dancing eyes and a bright smile "Nella. She keeps asking us for a brother or sister."

"Will you give her one?"

"Nella was adopted," Emory said, matter-of-factly, "I couldn't have children naturally. But we're thinking about adopting again." She grinned at Dante. "Just depends on whether my old man has the energy."

Dante laughed. "Enough with the 'old man'." He looked at Atom. "And what about you?"

Atom shrugged and told them about the divorce. "It was for the best."

"So recent though." Emory frowned at him. "Are you okay?"

No. No, I'm not okay. Not by a long shot. "I'm fine. Start of a new era." He looked at Dante. "Maybe you can suggest a new project for us to do together? I need a new challenge."

Dante and Emory exchanged a glance, and Dante nodded. "I'm sure we can come up with something."

"Atom... when we're settled in the new house, you'll have to come and stay with us for a weekend. If we ever find somewhere. We're looking at places out on Bainbridge Island."

"I can help with that," he told them. "I have contacts in the area."

AFTER HE'D SAID goodbye to his friends, he intended to drive home but instead drove into the city to one of his favorite clubs —a club that asked their clients to wear masquerade eye masks for the ultimate anonymity. He sat at the bar for a while before being welcomed into the rooms at the back of the club. It was another bar, but this time, the clientele wasn't there for cocktails.

As Atom fixed the masquerade mask over his eyes, he passed his gaze over the women there. He had already slept with a few of them, and some of them, he knew, wouldn't mind revisiting their trysts, but he never slept with the same woman twice—he'd made that known right at the beginning.

His eyes were drawn to a dark-haired woman seated at the bar. She was new. Her curves were poured into a skin-tight red dress which clung to her small waist and rounded hips. Her breasts were full and beautifully shaped. Atom felt his cock respond to her beauty. Her face was almost completely obscured by her white mask, but he could see her full, rose-pink mouth as she sipped her drink.

He went over, ordered a mineral water and sat down next to her. She didn't look at him, and when she picked her glass up, he could see her hands trembling. Ah. So, she was really new... and inexperienced at this.

"Hello."

She turned unnaturally violet eyes to him—contacts, he guessed. She really didn't want anyone to see the real her and that intrigued him. "Hello." A soft voice, a slight quaver.

He smiled, his eyes soft. "You're new here."

She nodded. "I am. I..." She gave a sweet little chuckle. "I don't really know what I'm doing here. It was a whim. I'm sorry, I should probably be all cool and confident, but the truth is... I have no idea what I'm doing." She shook her head, smiling. "I think I'm out of my depth here. I was just trying something different, you know? Something out of my comfort zone."

Atom touched a finger to her cheek, was gratified when she didn't pull away. There was something compelling about this woman, about her honesty. Usually, the people at the club put on an act—which was kind of the point of the masks—but this woman...

"If you're not comfortable, lovely lady..."

"I should go."

Atom felt bereft, but he nodded. "I would hate it if you were caught up in something you weren't ready for."

What was he saying? When had he turned into a bleeding heart? But something about her made him feel protective. She was gorgeous, sexy... and definitely in the wrong place. "May I walk you out?"

She hesitated, then nodded, and he offered her his arm. "I have to say, I'm surprised to find such a gentleman here. Thank you."

"You're welcome." *Ask her for her number. Ask her to come home with you. Don't let her go.* "Can I drive you home?"

Uh oh, wrong thing to say. He saw wariness in her eyes, and he held up his hands. "Forget I said that, I'm sorry. I meant it well, not as the awkward come-on it sounded like."

She gave a small laugh of relief. "It's okay, I'll take a cab."

Atom waited outside the club with her until they hailed a cab, then opened the door for her. "It was good to meet you."

"And you. Thank you rescuing me from that place." She hesitated then quickly kissed him, brief, soft on the mouth. "For what it's worth, you made this evening a good one. Goodbye."

"Bye."

He watched as the cab drove away and shook his head. What a freaking weird night. When the cab had disappeared into the night, Atom took off his mask, showing it into his pocket. He'd lost the enthusiasm for casual sex tonight. He went to his car, thankful he hadn't had anything alcoholic to drink. He wanted to drive in the cool air of the night to clear his head. His lips still tingled from the soft kiss, her soft kiss...

"Ah, damn it." What was wrong with him? Twice now, he'd

been in the company of a woman who had aroused in him not just sexual feelings, but something else, something deeper, and both times he'd let her go.

Fuck.

Maybe it was time to grow up and try to find someone who meant something more than a quick hook-up, someone he could really care about.

Maybe it was time.

CHAPTER FIVE

Maia thanked the cab driver and let herself into her hotel room. She stripped out of the red dress, and with relief, removed the violet contacts from her eyes. She was still trembling and when she'd showered and changed into sweats, she crawled onto the bed and let out a sigh.

"What the hell was I thinking?" Earlier, feeling brave—and frustrated—going to the club had seemed like a good idea. She had needed to feel the touch of another human, had needed it for a couple of years now, and tonight, her frustration had peaked, and she'd done her research on the internet.

Anonymous, masked sex sounded kinky and a good option. Maybe if the guy in the club hadn't been so kind, she would have gone through with it. She smiled to herself then. Yeah, he'd been a sweetie, and thank God for it.

Maia sat back against the headboard. At least she'd been saved from a train wreck. Her biggest train wreck of course was her life now. After five years of nothing but searching for Luka and Zach, not believing her daughter was gone, her friends had sat her down.

Sakata, Julia... they'd both told her some harsh truths.

"They're gone," Sakata had said, holding Maia's hands. "Luka is gone. Dead, Maia. Zach's note made that clear."

Maia winced now recalling it, but she had known they were right. "You need to make a new life now, my darling," Julia, who'd become a good friend, told her. "Away from New York."

She had known they were right about that, too. Her nemesis Tracey had been crowing to anyone who would listen about how Maia couldn't keep her husband happy, that she'd made him so desperate he killed himself and his daughter. There was more than one occasion when Maia had been held back from going full medieval on Tracey's smug ass. The final straw was the article in one of New York's high-end magazines. The article was clearly planted by Tracey and painted Maia as nothing more than a gold-digging whore. Maia's friend leapt to her defense and encouraged her to sue the writer and the magazine, but Maia was exhausted by all of it.

So, she'd chosen to move across the country. She'd never been to Seattle before, but as soon as she saw the waters of Elliott Bay and Puget Sound, the Olympic mountains, and Mount Rainier so majestic against the skyline, she knew she had made the right decision.

A new life.

The New York police were still refusing to close the case and declare Zach and Luka dead.

Zach... she would never forgive him. *Ever.* It was as simple as that. When, at his memorial, his friends had extolled on what a great man he was, she could hardly stop herself from screaming out that he was a murderer. That he had taken her daughter away—ended her young life for no other reason than to cause Maia pain.

Bastard.

So, Maia, her anger, her hurt a burning thing, divorced Zach *in absentia*, and in her divorce filing asked for sole custody of

Luka... the daughter who was lost. Zach's money was tied up, but she'd had enough saved of her own—and the apartment had been in her name for tax reasons—that she sold everything, readying for the move out to the West Coast.

She'd given Henry full control of Zach's part in the company, not caring to run it herself, but wanting to save some of Luka's inheritance... just in case.

Everything was 'just in case,' but with every day that passed, Maia began to accept she would never see her daughter again.

Now, she had been in Seattle for a few days, and for the time being, she had holed up in a small but clean hotel. She had some vague idea about what she wanted to do, but she'd lost confidence in herself. After the disappearance, she had given up her position at the publishing company, spending every day searching for any clue to Luka's fate.

She'd driven herself half mad.

Now, as she began to accept that Luka was gone, and as she stood on the edge of a new life, there was a small glimmer of optimism in her soul. There were good people in this world; the stranger at the sex club had proved that.

Two days later, she was standing in an empty storefront on Bainbridge Island. From the large picture windows, she could see across the bay to the city. The polished wooden floors and shelves smelled wonderful, and Maia knew she had found her place. She talked about the lease with the realtor and ended up signing a five-year contract.

"What will you do with the place?" The realtor, Jensen, was looking at her with interest, a cute young man with dark blonde hair and merry green eyes.

"A bookshop," she said, smiling at him. "I know that must sound boring to you, but I love reading."

"Not at all," he assured her. "I'm a nerd, too. Oh, I mean... no offense." He seemed to realize she might take that as an insult, but Maia laughed.

"None taken, I am a nerd and proud of it." She looked around her new premises. "Now, business done. Let's talk about somewhere to live."

JENSEN CAME through for her again with a home: he found her a small house on a quiet street with a garden that led down to a tiny private beach. It had been up for rent for a while, the furniture covered in dust sheets, but as Maia walked through it, she could see herself here.

The porch had an old swing, rife with woodworm, but as she sat down gingerly, it swung gently. Jensen was watching her. "Well?"

She smiled at him. "Yes. You had a good day, Jensen."

He laughed. "Glad to hear it. Now, let's get the business out of the way. I know some movers if you need them."

"I don't. I didn't bring anything but my clothes and books with me." Maia stood up. "I'm starting over, Jensen. But if you could point me in the way of a good furniture store, I'd be grateful."

A WEEK later and she had moved in. She found she enjoyed living so sparsely, so when Jensen had hooked her up with a great furniture store, she bought a few pieces—a new bed, kitchen table, some comfortable armchairs—but she found herself each evening sitting outside on the rickety porch swing and watching the sunsets over the island.

During the days she scrubbed, polished, and oiled the wooden floors and shelves of her new bookstore, and then enthusiastically filled the shelves. She sought out a sign maker and three weeks after her arrival in Washington, *Luka's Books*, opened to a curious crowd of buyers.

Atom hugged Emory as she opened the door to him. "Hey, you. You look... better." She studied him and nodded approvingly. Atom grinned at her. Even though they hadn't known each other for a long time, he'd grown very fond of his friend's wife.

Emory Harper had been through the mill when it came to life. Injured in a school massacre, she'd been shot by a vengeful ex-husband and only survived due to Dante's help and care. A former school teacher, she now taught as a professor at UW.

Nella, the Harpers' daughter, greeted Atom shyly. "I think she has a crush on you," Emory grinned to her daughter's protest.

Dante clapped Atom's shoulder. "Just in time. I've been cooking."

"Baby. You put steaks on a grill." Emory chuckled at his pout. "Okay, okay, that counts."

In the garden of their rented home on Bainbridge Island, Atom saw they had indeed started a cookout. Some mutual friends had also made their way to the party, and Atom chatted easily with them.

Emory was right. For the past few weeks, a weight had lifted from Atom's shoulders. No more was the fear of disappointing his father in his life... because the fear of disappointing himself had replaced it.

But that was something he could do something about. He'd been talking to Dante, late into the nights sometimes, and Dante had convinced him that change was already in his own hands.

He'd confided about the girl at the club, and Dante had nodded. "Sometimes people are brought into our lives for a reason. I know Em was, despite the horrific way we met. Em will tell you that everything happens for a reason, and she would know." He patted his friend's shoulder. "This girl, whoever she was, you may never see her again. You probably won't see her again. But just maybe, she taught you that someone could get into that heart of yours."

Atom had thought about his friend's words again and again between then and now, and in his everyday life, he began to see new possibilities, new connections he could make. He wasn't seeking 'the one' relentlessly, just opening his mind to something more than just a fling.

Certainly more than what he had given Gail during their marriage. Christ, he'd been a bastard even if he'd never raised his voice or his fist to her. Absence was another kind of abuse. He'd called her and left her a long rambling voicemail message when she didn't pick up, apologizing, but she hadn't called him back. Atom couldn't blame her. She wanted to move past the pain, and he could respect that. It wasn't for Gail to absolve his guilt.

"Hey, buddy." Dante sat down next to him now, beer in hand. "Now that I have a moment off from chef-ing duties—" he grinned as Emory scoffed at him, "I wanted to talk to you about something."

"Go for it."

"We've found some land here on the island, and we'd like you to build us a house."

Atom sipped his beer. "Oh, just that?" He laughed. "Wow, okay..."

"You're the best architect I know, hell, any of us know, and you've spent far too long sitting in meetings and behind desks. Come on, At, you know that's true. With all due respect, your father never gave you the freedom to create like I know you can. So, *carte blanche*. Unlimited budget. Build my girls a palace."

Atom grinned at his friend. "I'm assuming you're speaking figuratively?"

"You know what I mean. Emory has a ton of ideas, so I'm sure she'll tell you all of them and then some." Dante leaned in and said in a stage-whisper, "I hate to tell you this, but Em has a project book stuffed with ideas. There are turrets, man, turrets!"

"I can *hear* you." Emory giggled and came to sit on his knee. "So, Atom, Dante's told you?"

"He has, and I'm looking forward to it." Atom smiled at the couple, watching them as they held each other. They were so close, so in sync with each other, and it made Atom's heart ache. Would he ever find someone like that?

As he drove home that night, he wondered if Dante and Emory were so close because they had been through hell together—actual life-and-death crap. He felt bad for feeling so depressed when they had been through much worse than he had ever been through...... that he would admit to, anyway. There were some parts of his life that he had closed off to himself and had denied all his life because they were just too painful to confront.

On the ferry back to the mainland, he looked back over to the island. He liked the pace of life there—it was pretty chill. It was a bedroom community, feeding into the city's businesses, yes, but he liked the feel of the place.

And it was beautiful, too. He was looking forward to building Dante and Emory's new home and while he was out there, maybe he'd rent a place—see how island life suited him.

It was something different. A different way to live his life. His business practically ran itself, thanks to his uber-efficient team, and it wasn't as if he couldn't afford to take time off for a passion project. Thanks to his father's will, he was worth billions.

Atom half-laughed to himself. He had made his own money, albeit with the help of a good education and help from his father, but now, with unlimited resources....

Just don't waste it, he told himself, *use it to build a new life, get some passion back.* Yes, this new project would change things for him, and it was about time.

With a definite lift in his spirits he went home and straight to bed, dreaming of blueprints, bricks, and a new life.

If you want to continue reading this story, you can get your copy from your favorite vendor by searching for the title:

While You Were Gone
A Christmas Second Chance Romance

You can also find the e-book version by typing this link in your computer's browser:

https://www.hotandsteamyromance.com/products/while-you-were-gone-a-christmas-second-chance-romance

OTHER BOOKS BY THIS AUTHOR

Saving Her Rescuer: A Billionaire & A Virgin Romance

I was just trying to get away from my crazy ex for the weekend when I ended up in a giant pileup on the highway up to Gore Mountain.

https://www.hotandsteamyromance.com/collections/frontpage/products/saving-her-rescuer-a-billionaire-a-virgin-romance

∼

Sensual Sounds: A Rockstar Ménage

Lust. Lies. Double lives.

The rock and roll industry is full of people who are looking out for themselves and willing to do anything to rise to the top.

https://www.hotandsteamyromance.com/collections/frontpage/products/sensual-sounds-a-rockstar-menage

∼

On the Run: A Secret Baby Romance

Murder. Lies. Fraud. Just another day in the lives of billionaires and women on the run.

https://www.hotandsteamyromance.com/collections/frontpage/products/on-the-run-a-secret-baby-romance

∽

<u>The Dirty Doctor's Touch: A Billionaire Doctor Romance</u>

I am a master. An elitist. I am at the top of my field, and I know what I am doing.

https://www.hotandsteamyromance.com/collections/frontpage/products/the-dirty-doctor-s-touch-a-billionaire-doctor-romance

∽

<u>The Hero She Needs: A Single Daddy Next Door Romance</u>

He's the only man I've ever wanted...

https://www.hotandsteamyromance.com/collections/frontpage/products/the-hero-she-needs-a-single-daddy-next-door-romance

∽

<u>If you want to see all of my books click here!</u>

https://www.hotandsteamyromance.com/

ABOUT THE AUTHOR

Mrs. Love writes about smart, sexy women and the hot alpha billionaires who love them. She has found her own happily ever after with her dream husband and adorable 6 and 2 year old kids.
Currently, Michelle is hard at work on the next book in the series, and trying to stay off the Internet.
"Thank you for supporting an indie author. Anything you can do, whether it be writing a review, or even simply telling a fellow reader that you enjoyed this. Thanks

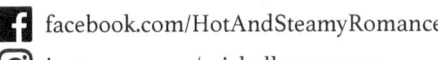

facebook.com/HotAndSteamyRomance
instagram.com/michellesromance

COPYRIGHT

©Copyright 2020 by Michelle Love - All rights Reserved
In no way is it legal to reproduce, duplicate, or transmit any part of this document in either electronic means or in printed format. Recording of this publication is strictly prohibited and any storage of this document is not allowed unless with written permission from the publisher. All rights are reserved.
Respective authors own all copyrights not held by the publisher.

www.ingramcontent.com/pod-product-compliance
Lightning Source LLC
LaVergne TN
LVHW021705060526
838200LV00050B/2505